SPLINTER

SPLINTER

A Novel in Verse

BETSY O'NEILL - SHEEHAN

ISBN:979-8-218-33597-7

First Printing, 2024

For all who have gone through obstacles and felt they had
to bend into someone else to get through, who felt they've
lost a piece of themselves, who wished they could go back
to another way of being.
You are everything you need to be.

For my family and friends,
who support all the fragments of me.

For Rob, who always believes in me.

1

Brewen

A Ray of Hope

There's a rainbow above me,
I just know it.
The sun bends
through the clouds
and glints off what's left
of the drops finishing up
this late August rainstorm.
It's there.

I just can't see it
through this ceiling I'm
under.

Steam rises with the scent
of streets washed clean
in this old paper mill of a town,
west of Springfield, Massachusetts.
On the edge of the Berkshire mountains,
it's named for the trees that
turned into envelopes and
fine writing paper.

Holyoke.

From our porch
three floors up
it looks like the water
level on the canal
raised about two inches
from just that one storm.
But even fish
don't want to swim
there.

Windows crack open all down

Appleton Street,
propped up by Bluetooth speakers.
A cool breeze breaks
the oppressive heat.
Children splash in puddles
and dance to the sound of
their own laughter
accompanied by the thump of
classic Daddy Yankee on repeat.
They keep their social distance,
at least six feet apart,
but they still jump
at the chance to play
together.

The rain has stopped enough
for me to set up
these frayed plastic lawn chairs
for a COVID friendly
meeting with my social worker.
My foster mother, Gina
has had these chairs
much longer than the
six years I've been here.
They can barely hold themselves
together.

"You know, you could
get some new chairs
for like five bucks
at Top Dollar."
I tease her.

She stands with half her body
propping the screen door open.
"They don't make those things
to last anymore.
These ones will probably last longer.

Anyway,
I don't get rid
of anything that
still has some hope in it."

I don't know if
she's still talking
about chairs,
or if she means
me.

"What time is Jandro coming?"
she asks.

The digital clock
on the bank across the way
glows a red 4:35pm.
"Five minutes ago,"
I shrug.

"That man, there's always something
he's got to take care of."

Sometimes that something
is someone.
Sometimes that someone
is me.

"Well, I'm off to the salon.
Mrs. P's got a 4:45.
Chris said he'll be at work late.
So, girl, you are on your own
for dinner.
I left a few dollars on the counter."

She pauses for a moment
and I think I see a tear well
in her eye, but

that can't be possible.
Gina's the toughest.
Strictest rules.
Grit to the bone.
I have never seen her cry.
She swallows so hard
her neck gets all bulgy.
She clears her throat
and pulls up her
work-issued N-95 mask.

"Tomorrow, let's have
coffee before I leave
for work."

And I know that's her way
of acknowledging that tomorrow,
August 28, 2021, is
my eighteenth birthday.
"Sounds good, G."

I never call Gina "mom"
that's just not how we roll.
Maybe someday I'll tell her
about how she gave me hope.
Kind of like a rainbow
I somehow knew was there
but couldn't always see.

With me turning eighteen
her foster care
duty is over.
She's not kicking
me out tomorrow
but pretty soon
I'll have to leave.

Set the Board

Jandro has brought
his busted old chess set
to every visit
we've had
since I was twelve.
He likes to pretend
that he lets me win,
but we both know
he's faking.
I'm going to miss him.
"You're in check,"
I say.

"I know, I know," he says
as he shifts in the lawn chair.
"You sure this chair will
hold me up?"
He's got a strong build,
makes the chair look small.

"They have every other time.
Gina says she still has hope in them."

"Well, that means something, then.
Doesn't it?
Just like she had hope in you.
And that all worked out."

There were
six fosters,
four schools,
and two hospitals,
before Gina
that didn't work out.
The BG Times, I call them
(as in Before Gina.)

My dark ages.

Jandro's eyes bounce
from the board
to a thick manilla envelope
planted next to his bag
on the card table
Gina uses for
Thursday night poker.
Either this is the most
important round of chess
Jandro's ever played
or there's a whole world
he's protecting
stuffed in that package.
He makes a mindless move,
advances a pawn
to a clear space
further away from conflict.
He does nothing to
try to win.

I take his king.

"Well, that's one way
to end our last game," I say.

Win or lose,
I promised myself
no tears today.

Which Game are We Playing?

We all have our different games.
Gina's a shark at *Five Card Draw*.
Sometimes "working late" means
she's gone to Springfield
to the casino.
She likes to make bets,
take chances,
like the chance
she took on me
taking me in at twelve
when everyone else said
they couldn't
"handle my episodes."

                  Jandro once told me how
                  he batted .300
                  in the minor leagues.
                  I'm not exactly sure
                  what that even means,
                  but if he's telling me
                  I think it must be good.
                  Baseball is a whole other
                  language he speaks.

                  All he's ever wanted
                  to do is get
                  me home safe.

Me?
I've never played anyone
I couldn't beat at chess
at least once.
I'm all about scoping out roles
and strategies,
reading who is with
and who is
against me.

All these games,
different rules,
different plays,
in the end
we all want to win,
or at least leave some kind of mark along the way.

Goodbye in the Language of Baseball

"Tomorrow's the big
birthday. I can't believe
you are already eighteen,"
Jandro says as he wiggles
the envelope out
from underneath
the discarded chess pieces.

A pawn rolls toward
the table's edge
but I save her before
she takes the leap
three floors down
to the sidewalk.

He doesn't notice
my great catch as
he's trying too hard
to avoid eye contact
with me from
behind the brim
of his Yankees hat.
Apparently,
neither of us,
is good at goodbyes.

"This is a big moment
for you. You're ready
to make your own way.
We've got some things set up
for you, of course.
Gina says you can stay
here until you are ready
to go."

"As long as I keep
it all together," I say

in my best no-nonsense
Gina-like tone.

"Hey, she's been good
for you," he laughs.

"Yeah, she has."
I laugh back
to cover up
my sad.
That's a goodbye
for another day.

"You know, this doesn't
have to be it.
You can change your mind
if you don't want to
be emancipated just yet.
DCF has things to support you
until you are twenty-two."

"Either way, this is
our last meeting,
right?"

"Well, yeah. But
I would transfer your case to – "

"I don't want to be transferred again.
And I'm tired of
being somebody's case."

"But you can get stipends for –"

"You told me already.
That's just money.
Hardly enough for anything.
Do you know how much
I'd be willing to pay
to
never
go
to
another

placement
again?
And where will I go?
With Gina?"

                                        "Well, no."

"Nah, I'm good."
/I sit back and/
/cross my arms/
/creating a barrier/
/between the world/
/and my heart./
My lawn chair
groans on my behalf.
Jandro leans forward
as if he is trying
to find a way
through my walls.

                              "I love Gina and all,
                         but she could up and decide,
                                              well,
                       whatever she decides someday."

"I get it.
It's just,
I've been
in this
my whole life.
My
whole
entire
life,
and I always promised
myself,
I'm out
the first chance
I get to be.
Not everybody is like
you, Jandro.
Not everybody helps."

"I know."
He positions the chess
pieces back in their start places.
"I just want
to make sure
I've done the best
I could for you.
Even if the system
doesn't always
make sense."
He pulls off his hat
and smooths the sweat
from off his head.

"I can't deal with any more
social workers.
No more fosters.
No more group homes.
I got to try to
do this
on my own."

He puts his hat
back on. It shields
his eyes.
"I get it.
And if anyone
can make it,
it'll be you.
Just please
remember
you have the
option to return."

I've got nothing else
to say on this.
I made my choice.
He knows where I stand.

"Ok, so, there's
something else
I know you've told me

you don't remember
a lot of things that happened..."
He looks down Appleton
as if the right words might
show up on the bank sign.

"Before Gina?
Yeah, it's a fog."

"Well, I don't want to walk
away today
without leaving you
with some answers.
I mean, if you ever
have questions."
He picks up the envelope
and taps it in his hand
like it's a baseball bat
and he's up next
to hit.
"But I also know
you have to do this
on your own time.
When you are ready.
If you want to."

"For when I am ready?
Do you think I will ever be?"
All I've ever been told
was watered down.
The rest
I can't
or don't
or won't
remember.
It's not his fault.
The doctors at the hospital
said that whenever I start
to remember
my body has a response

like an allergy.
I go into some sort
of emotional anaphylaxis,
a personal protection system
in my brain
because it doesn't want
to go through
those memories again.
Those memories are
stronger than my meds,
My pulse beats like
I should be running
from one base to the next.
But I'm not sure
how to play this game.

"I know. I know.
It's hard.
But it's your story,
the pieces of it that were
shared with me, anyway.
That's why I want you to
put this somewhere safe
in case you ever
want to
or ever need
to know more."

He hands the envelope
to me, as if I'm
up last
and he trusts me
to bat for myself.

We All Start with a Name

There was a name for me
once upon a long time ago
in the Times BG.
The one I began with,
the one my mom sang
when she'd rock me to sleep.
Or at least, I hope she did.
I don't really know.

As Jandro leaves
through Gina's apartment,
I'm frozen on the porch
staring down the envelope
that seals the stories
of all the things
that happened to me.
Of my real name,
a faded memory,
abandoned in
the foster home
just before this one.
Tomorrow, I turn eighteen
so, this
is really it for me.
These papers
officially release me
from the custody
of the Massachusetts Department of
Children and Families.
For when I'm ready?
Will I ever be?

This soulless package,
all my personal baggage,
is an anchor in my hands,

a weight that holds me
where I am
and won't let me
move
from here.
My heart plummets
down,
down,
down,
and sinks into the sand
of the darkest gray depths
of my memories.
Where there are so many stories of
so many faces,
so many names,
that came in and out of my life.
I can't remember them all so
I just call them "They."

They (In the Times BG)

I don't know why she chose to leave.
They tell me it was an act of love,
that my mother knew her own barriers,
so, she left me in that baby carrier
at the safe haven,
the Hospital of the Shining Dove.
They found me
where my bio mom left me
just a baby girl on the floor
in the emergency room
of the same hospital
where she delivered me
into this world.

They/Them:
the nurses who fed me,
the social workers who guarded me,
the fosters who fed/clothed/bathed
and some even came close to loving me.
Teachers.
Doctors.
Counselors.
Those people who gave me rides to my appointments.
Police.
Lawyers.
Therapists.
In and out of my story as the years go on,
there are really too many to list.

All I ever wanted
was just one or two
who would stay
with me all the way.

Let it Go

They thought it'd be safer for me
if I let it   go.
    Let it all go.

Let go of
all the things
I saw,
all the things
I was.
They even wanted me
to forget my name.
Shove it all away
and walk
on
              like
nothing
ever
happened.

But They were confused,
because I didn't let it go.
It
  let
    go
      of
        me.
And left me with a picture inside my head
but I don't know what it is.
Scattered pieces of memories
keep
    folding
and unfolding
in my mind
  like an infinite grid,
  a beam of light

caught in a spectrum
of confusion,
   and I don't know what
         color I'm in.
I never considered
that color could be
manilla like this
unfeeling
standardized
package.

I set it on the linoleum counter
on top of the rest of
Gina's mail
and her salon product catalogs,
more comfortable not knowing
all the things
I've come to forget,
at least for now.
It's easier thinking
that it's all coincidence.
All my life I've survived
on chains of co-incidents.
The good that comes with the bad.
The hope inside tragedy.
The people who run to help,
like the ones who threw safety nets to me,
and pulled me in
even if
only
for
a
moment.

I either
live this life,
   or
      slip

into
    a
       dream.
Can't take for granted
that things are
          always
            as
          they
       seem.
There are a million others
who swim down this same stream.
   But when it comes down to it,
   it feels like
   it's just me,
   and that's a lonely place to be.

   But lonely
   was the only place
   that ever really felt safe.
   I didn't
   couldn't
   wouldn't truly let myself love
   until I met my Destiny.

   No really, she's a person
   whose name is
   Destiny.

An Encounter with Destiny

Six years ago,
at the sixth-grade trip
to the science museum's
invasive aquatic life exhibit,
I sat on a bench
like any new kid to their fifth school:
quiet and alone.
Through the looking glass
fish swam past
in schools,
none of them alone.
From the outside looking in
I couldn't tell which of them
was bad or good. They seemed
to coexist.

The light shifted
as they drifted
into the shadow of the
reflection of a new girl.
Destiny fell into my path,
not figuratively,
but literally,
pretty darn awkwardly.
And for the first time
in a long time
I let my guard down
and genuinely laughed.

                    "You have a nice smile," she said
                              as she nudged
                         her way onto the bench.
I couldn't help but
smile more as my heart made
some room for her, too.

Now six years later
she's the only one
who gets me.
And she looks back at me
with eyes of love
like she knows
where I'm going
so it doesn't much matter
where I've been.

I am Brewen
and I'm brewing
into something
now that my
Destiny
has a name.

Almost 18

Most kids dream of eighteen.
For them it's piercings, voting, and scratch tickets,
all kinds of lucid freedoms
that smell like CBD gummies and e-cigarettes.
That "if you fail" kind of independence
where you have a family to fall back on.
Take chances.
No regrets.

But I'm just a day away
from my eighteenth birthday.
And eighteen for fosters
means I have the opportunity
for emancipation,
as in they
set me free.
Free, like I've never
had the chance to be.
Free from abuse,
neglect, all those things
that happened to me
that I'd rather not remember.

I choose that freedom so
"They" will be done with me.
"They" will no longer be there
because "They" don't have to be.
"They" won't owe me anymore.
"They" won't own me anymore
and as much as this should be a relief...
I mean...
this is what I want
but...
this aging out freedom
has me on my knees,

terrified
of independence.
Because independence by definition
is on your own,
as in "alone"
like an empty bed,
an empty family tree.
Empty like this bed
where I can lay my head
and wonder every night,
"Is this my last night?

Who knows how long Gina
will keep putting up with me?
When the clock strikes eighteen
I will get this life right.
Because I have to.
I have nothing to go back to.
Time moves straight ahead.
It doesn't stop.
It doesn't bend.
It doesn't go back to change memories
or histories.
The future is the only place for me.

2

Destiny

1,2,3

There are three things
I will miss
when I leave for college
tomorrow.
If only I could
figure out a way
to take a piece
of them with me.

1

Summer sounds in these city streets after the rain.

Music, laughing, dancing.

*Solution: Upload Daddy Yankee for when I need
the pulse of the streets.*

2

Sunsets over the canal, especially ones with rainbows like today.

They remind me that the world is bigger
than this apartment building,
and so much more
than me.

*Solution: Slip my old crystal unicorn into my pocket
to take some rainbows with me.*

3

The people I love:

Pa   Ma
Brewen

Solution:

(This space left intentionally blank.)

I guess the hardest part is that

they
stay here
while
I
leave.

Full Scholarship

Room.
Board.
Tuition.
All student expenses paid
at the University of Vermont
courtesy of:

a whole lot of dedication,
finishing my AP Bio lab reports
on the bench
outside the McDonald's
around the block,
catching enough Wifi
into the wee hours of the night,

a whole lot of good decisions,
the kinds that make me leave
a party when I am having fun
but before fun turns
into trouble,

a whole lot of intuition,
listening to my heart
and the people who
look out for me.

But Will There Ever Be

anyone who watches
out for me
like Brew?

How will I say goodbye to her?

Dear Brewen,

Tomorrow is so
BIG
for us. Like
ALL
the things we
EVER
wanted are coming
TRUE.
But I don't
WANT
to have to say
GOODBYE.
Or to be another person who
LEFT

YOU

get to be done with
all the things you've
ever wanted to forget.

Case closed.

Me

a whole damn staircase

you helped me build

toward dreams

with each small step

We Both

knew this day was coming.

I Wish

it didn't come so soon.

I don't want to leave you.

3

Brewen

How Much Does it Cost to Choose?

I grab the five dollars
Gina left me on the counter.
My allowance for dinner.
Pretty soon the state
will stop their stipends
and I will
have to foot
my own bill.

    That's ok.
I chose that.
I *chose* that.
I made a decision about my own life.

I'll make another:
I'll get a job soon.

As I walk past Top Dollar
I wonder if I should
take these dollars
and buy Gina
one of those lawn chairs
as a joke.

But my stomach disagrees.
So I choose to eat.

I pull up my disposable surgical mask
in these unprecedented COVID times.
    That's my choice, too.

Trauma (With a Big T)

A stop at the grocery store
shouldn't be too complicated.
Mask up,
go in,
buy instant ramen,
get out.

The arrows taped on the floor
to ensure social distancing
add a layer of predictability.
I don't even have to speak
to anyone I don't want to.
(And trust me,
I don't want to.)

   But sometimes my body remembers
things my mind forgets:
   like how I get nauseous at the
smell of bananas.
   or how I freeze at the sight of
   a crying child.

   How I want to run
        from men's voices
             and especially their eyes.

                              "That'll be $4.35,
                    The checkout attendant says
                            as if it's the third time.
                         Maybe it's the third time.
                            I think I didn't hear her
            because I was trapped somewhere else
                                        in my mind.

I hand her the five-dollar bill.
She winces as she accepts the cash
and hurries back my $.65
like she's trying to abide
by some kind of three - second - rule.

As if we can get a virus to follow any of our rules.

The Fire

Foster home number seven
hasn't been the worst
but it's certainly no heaven.
Gina works so hard
to barely make ends meet.
She works late hours
so, most of the time
I'm on my own
for lunch and dinner.

Her partner, Chris,
he came around after
she got me.
Ragged like those
old lawn chairs,
but she must see
some kind of
hope in him.

Chris and I don't talk much,
like we have a silent agreement
that we are both around
to make Gina happy.
Sometimes it's like
between the channels
radio static
when our eyes meet.
So, I make sure we're never alone.

But sometimes we're alone.

Today's dinner is ramen on the gas lit stove.

He asks, "A little hot for ramen, no?"

I didn't realize he was home.

Trigger terror inside me
that screams,
scalds,
thrashes,
and throws.

A forcefield in my mind
traps me inside
where I'm no longer in control.
My feeling gets so big
so fast
it
E
   X
      P
    L
      O
    D
      E
        S,
and it doesn't matter
what or who
is in my path.
My body can't
        contain it.
My brain can't
        reframe it.
I'm unaware of all
that happens
until I see the
AfTeRMaTh.

I can't remember a single thing
until that blaring sound in my ears rings
like some bomb in a movie went off.
But there is no movie.

and I'm the bomb.

When I come to
my hands and arms burn.

"What are you doing?" he yells,
his voice shaking,
scared,
and concerned.

I sit outside myself
watching me
watching him.
My body seems lifeless,
like it's on pause,
and I try to tell myself
to move,
to feel,
to think.

At the hospital they called these moments
DiSaSSoCiAtioNs.

The air is crisp
but not like cool fresh spring,
more like crispy burnt hair.
Extinguisher foam coats the linoleum counter,
the pile of mail,
and apparently,
my hair.

Finally, my body responds
to my brain's commands to move.
My hand drags through the fizzling froth
of my tangled locks.
With a clean dish towel
Chris covers my burns.

This wasn't him.
It was me,
or at least some kind
of echoed fragment
of me revisiting
from somewhere
in my past.

"Are you alright?"
His voice is kindness,
but I'm still in shock
as my body lifts itself off the floor.

I run my fingers through
the charred ruins
of the envelope on the counter,
leaving a
hot,
messy,
mark
of ashes
in my path.

Lifting my fingers
to my lips
I taste the ash.
Bitter like poison.
There was nothing good
for me in there.
Anything that was good
I can still remember.

Chris doesn't say it yet,
like he knows I can't
handle it,
but I think I know.
He doesn't have to say the words.
What I read in his eyes says enough.

He's scared.
Gina and Chris
won't want me here
anymore.

My whole history,
just burned.

Flight

My body runs from
the dangers it perceives.
Away from the house,
from Chris,
that look in eyes.

Away from the fire engines
rolling up the road,
sirens blaring,
rushing
toward danger
to assess the damage.

Away from Gina
discovering
her new subway kitchen tiles
charred with burnt noodles,
knowing the extra hours
she'll have to work
to replace them.

Away from the possibility
that they will
have to send me
to another
group home
or hospital.

Away from the fire
that was my past.

I run until I escape
that moment
and all of its
sights and sounds,

but I can never run
fast enough
to escape
myself.

I run to the only place
where I feel safe.

I run to Destiny.

Let Me In?

> "I'm here for you," Destiny says
> like a whisper in my heart.

Her empathy forces through my floodgates
as I stumble through her door.

Splinter

"This is my reality
and tomorrow you'll go
so far away from me.
Destiny, I started a fire.
My whole life feels like misery.
I can see why they
wanted me
to forget
about me.
I think I'm broken
I don't even really know what happened.
My memory turns gray
and I can't step away.
until I wake.

And I can't remember
how the ramen ended up on the floor
or the pot across the room
or the fire up the wall
and if it was his fault or mine.
But I know it was mine.
Why does this happen to me all the time?"

I sigh a sharp,

splintered,

shattered

sigh.

Even my sighs are broken.

Breathe – *Destiny*

"You don't need to say a word.
Stay here in this room.
Don't have to explain your hurt.

Just stay here and breathe

with me."

Wash it Out

Destiny washes my hair
in the bathroom sink
Warm water soothes,
draining away the smokey burning stink.
Ash and soot flow out
with each tender wring
of water calming the fire
that burns my soul.

She looks through the foggy mirror back at me.
My breathing ebbs with hers.
She dries my face
and I see my dark eyes in hers
as with each loving touch
she wipes away
my running mascara.

        "You're not broken," she says.
        "And you won't be forgotten.
        You're staying with me."

"I can't do that.
You know I can't.
I've got nowhere I can be."
One more night until 18
and absolutely
nobody
wants
 me.

        "I told you.
        You're staying here tonight."
        She says in a way that feels like home.

"What about your parents?

I know they
want you to
move on and
forget about me."

               "We'll hide you away.
            They won't have to know."

"But you have to
leave for college."

           "So, I guess you'll have to come."

"But Destiny – "

            "We'll sneak you in my dorm.
                 It's a single.
            Everyone will think that
                I'm alone."

"We were supposed to
say goodbye tonight,
so you could do this
on your own.
You deserve all the things
you worked so hard for.
You shouldn't have to
worry about me anymore."
Blood, soot, soap, water,
all flow away together.
A stream of mess
swirls down the drain
leaving me
wet, burnt, clean.

             "I can't leave you.
              Not like this."
          She wraps a fresh towel

around me.
"You stay with me."

"Are you sure about this?
Where will I go?"

"I always find you," she says
then pulls out her trifold campus map.
"There," she points.
"That's the dorm.
I'll find you on a bench outside.
I will always find you."

"I don't know.
I don't want to
risk your chance
to follow your dreams.
But I will hide away here tonight.
We can figure it out
tomorrow."
I have no more words for her,
just tears that wash it
all
down
hard.
Her love fills me up
and seams together all my
scattered,
		splintered
				shards.

Trouble Brewen

The smell of coffee
leaks through the bedroom door
waking us.
Destiny goes to the kitchen,
each step creaking
on the worn floor boards
of the old mill-town apartment.
Through the thin walls
where she's concealed me,
I hear parent voices.

"We know this will be good for you.
It'll be good for you to go.
Start fresh.
Start new.
Away from the troubles here, you know?
What we mean to say
is maybe you need a little distance
from this trouble, Brewen.
Maybe you could try
to fly
a little on your own.
But please know that
we believe in you
and we'll be here
when you're ready
to come home."

A Cup of Brew

"See? You heard them!"
I whisper with the intensity
of a serious librarian.

                        "Heard them?" she asks.

"Fly a little *on your own*
Away from *this trouble, Brewen.*"
She folds up the comforter
from her bed, and packs it
in a trash bag. The pillow
she throws directly
at my head.

                        "I don't think that's
                        what they meant."

"They're right, you know.
You should go on your own.
I'll make it easier.
I'm leaving you.
You aren't leaving me.
You don't need that kind
of guilt when you have a
future to build."
Maybe she doesn't hear me,
or maybe she
just doesn't take me seriously
because she laughs.

                    "Where exactly are you going to go?"
                              she asks.
                    "I told you, you won't be forgotten.
                        I'm not leaving you behind."

"You really think
we can make this work?"

"I know we have to try."

Packing List - *Destiny*

A comforter - two pillows - a charger for her phone -
Clothes – masks - shoes - coats - boots -
Stationary to send notes home -
A journal - debit card - bathroom toiletries
A game of chess
School supplies - computer - medication - miscellaneous stuff we need

Packing List - *Brewen*

Anything of mine that's still at Destiny's:
My toothbrush, - a change of clothes -
Thank God there's extra underwear in there
my backpack - my black hoodie -
and *Civil Disobedience* by Henry David Thoreau

How Are We Going to Do This?

"Do you really want to do this?
How will we make it work?"

"Remember when I went away
for that freshman orientation earlier this year?
So many people still wear face masks in this
2021 post (maybe not post) COVID atmosphere.
just tie yours up and pretend you're me."

She moves me to the mirror,
pulls my hair back like hers,
attaches a face mask over
my mouth and nose.

"See?"

"I guess I can't disagree.
But what about your scholarship?"

"What do you mean?"

"Having me there, with you.
That would break the rules.
You'd lose your scholarship.
That's the only way you could afford –"

"We'll make it work,"
she says like it's the final word.

Her eyes are big and brown like mine,
except hers don't have a lens of pain.
There's hope and trust
in life and us.
She sees colors

while I see gray.

For her, the world is covered
in shallow waters,
full of light, and
soothing.

For me,
fires burn deep
in my defensive heart,
planning our next moves.

For her, the world is a
natural laboratory
of
harmony
and interdependence.

For me,
the world is
played like a game
of chess
where the pieces have
their
hierarchy
and codependence.

Loaded Up

It's wild to see how many things
a 2012 Subaru can fit,
and still have room for three people.
Destiny's dad reasons spatially
as her mom stands by impatiently
continuously adding

"Just one more thing,"

"Ma," says Destiny,
"that's enough to bring."

"But your medication, Honey.
Don't forget the Alprazolam.
It's in the front pocket of your duffle bag.
Oh, and set a daily reminder
and remember,
drink lots of water."

I can hear Destiny's eyes roll
as they take one last walk around the car
to make sure it's all crammed in.
Then they set off on their way to UVM.

4

Destiny

On the Road

"Red –
      Orange –
            Yellow –
                  Green –
                        Blue –
                              Indigo –
                                    Violet,"

I mutter these
quietly
to ease
the panic
rising
in my
veins.
Organization,
preoccupation,
routines, and repetition
hush my limbic system.
Something about the predictability
gives order
to the world
for me.

Red–for the color
of Ma's hair
blowing in the wind
from the open crack
in the window
of the Subaru.

Orange–for the color
of Pa's right shoe
slamming the brake
while some guy

tailgates us
on the Vermont Interstate.
"Masshole!"
he yells at the
guy with Massachusetts plates
giving us a one-fingered wave
while speeding past us
in the breakdown lane.

Yellow–
That one's easy.
The sun.
As long as it's not rainy,
or cloudy,
or night,
I always have that one.

Green–my favorite–
the color
of the earth.
Green mountains roll on
and on and
kiss the

Blue–sky.

Indigo–
Indigo–
Oh, shit here we go...
I can't find something indigo.

My watch warns
that my heart rate's up,
and it's time for me to breathe.
The little cyber flower
blooming on the screen
is a violet.

Which would be great
if I was on violet.

But I'm on indigo.
Red – Orange - Yellow – Green – Blue – Indigo - Violet
Red – Orange - Yellow – Green – Blue – Indigo - Violet
Red – Orange - Yellow – Green – Blue – Indigo - Violet
Red – Orange - Yellow – Green –

Everything turns gray.

Deep Dive

My brain slips further in the gray.
Sometimes it's an empty,
shallow
pool of stillness,
the kind of shallow
you don't want
to plunge headfirst into.
These panics should come
with a disclaimer.

WARNING: NO DIVING
Could cause injury
or even death.

Sometimes there is no warning
before I sink
beyond the places where light
penetrates the water,
beyond the schools of life
swimming,
to where it is
lifeless,
dark,
and gray.

Sometimes it's a memory
that takes my thoughts to
another time and space
while my body waits,
an unresponsive
shell of me
in present time.

Rainbow Memory:

Erasing the "D" in "Destiny"
compulsively,
it was either too fat
or too lopsided,
too dark,
or too light,
almost like this name,
D-E-S-T-I-N-Y,
wasn't even mine.
"I just can't get it right."
Not the right my brain wanted it to be.
My thoughts have a habit
of getting stuck on me.
My new sixth grade teacher
watched me as I muttered,
"Red – Orange - Yellow – Green – Blue – Indigo -Violet."
Over,
and over,
and over,
and over.
She was the first one
to notice
I wasn't delaying
or avoiding
what was asked of me.
I was captured
in a cycle
of my anxiety.

"Tell me what's happening,"
she said gently.

"The rainbow, the colors,
they keep me from the gray."
My pencil eraser wore

64

down to the bare metal tip.

Tears in the paper erased my letters.
Tears from my eyes erased my words.

She went to
her desk
and fumbled through
the top drawer.
Circling back to me
with a keychain
of a crystal unicorn.

"Watch this," she said
as she cast a spectrum
like a spotlight
on my "D."

My very own personal rainbow

With Me All the Way

I kept my crystal unicorn
with me all the time.
So much,
that the horn broke off
in the wash
when I forgot it
in my pocket
again.
So, I guess,
technically,
it became a crystal horse.

On our sixth-grade field trip,
sitting on the bench
in front of the aquarium
of fish life of Lake Champlain,
I casted spectrums on the viewing glass,
and caught them in my hand.
Warm light danced
and tickled my skin
like actual magic in this world
that kept me from the gray.
Fish followed the light
and shadows of
kids running in and out
of the exhibit rooms.
One bumped into my arm.
One kid, that is,
not a fish.

My horse
who was once
a unicorn,
took flight
and transformed

into a Pegasus.
I tried to catch
but missed
and fell
into a new girl.
Through the reflection,
Brewen smiled
like she knew who I was.
And she felt oddly,
so vaguely familiar,
like she was a friend
from the past,
like I stepped into my own rainbow,
a determined light
shining through the rain.

Pegasus

I still keep the old keychain
buried in my bag
just in case.
As long as there's Brewen
I don't really need it.
But sometimes it's fun
to play with the light.

Sun shines through the crystal
spilling spectrums from the ceiling
of the car
to the floor.
I skate them in figure eights
on the palms of my hands,
like I'm catching infinity
or hope
or those things that people
are always chasing
to convince themselves
that life is more
than what it seems.

I shift the colors onto Ma's sleeping head.

Pa looks back at me and says,
"You know we are really going to miss you,
and all the silly shit you do."

Through the rearview I try to tell him
that it's not quite time yet
for goodbyes.
But nothing comes out.
My heart isn't good
at goodbyes.
I don't know why we call them good.

The spectrums wander out the window
and shine against the advertisement
of Pegasus flying past us
on the wall of a bus.
Somewhere behind the tinted windows
Brewen is making her way
up to Vermont.
As I look at my warped reflection
I wonder if
maybe she is looking back at me, too.

5

Brewen

College Town

The University of Vermont
in the hub of Burlington
looks down from the top of the hill
toward sprawling Lake Champlain.
And in between, here and there
Church Street buzzes
with all its artsy culture and shops.
That's where the bus stops,
at the station at Church and Cherry.
I make my way up Pearl Street
to the university's Central Campus Hall.

Of all these hundreds of faces
there's only one I care to see.
She's probably somewhere inside
unloading all the things
from the 2012 Subaru.
Her parents won't want to see me so
I'll wait on this bench
just over here,
just like we planned,
opposite to a silent dude in a green shirt
where I can see everyone come and go.

Hidden in my mask
they all walk on past,
the hive of hundreds
moving in
to this college town.
They're all caught up in their long goodbyes.
Kids promise certainty as their mothers cry
like it's the first day of kindergarten
but reversed.
This time it's the moms struggling to part.
Just one more

one last kiss.

Pretty soon,
when all the Subaru's depart
in the great white exodus of SUVs
the kids will finally be
a little more like me:
on their own,
without their families.

The Literacy of Reading People

I don't have a phone,
one of the residual effects
of fending on my own.
But it keeps my Spidey-senses keen.
There are people and scenery to read.
Reading people's faces
is a special kind of literacy.

Like this dude in the green shirt
who runs his hands through his
mid-length hair
as if he cares if he looks cool
but wants to be cool enough
not to care.
This guy who still hasn't said a word,
whose eyes follow every pretty girl,
what could he possibly be waiting for?

She Finds Me

Somehow,
even if I'm lost in a crowd
or somewhere deep inside
chasing thoughts,
she finds me.
She pierces through
like hopeful sunlight,
rays hitting just right.
And if she told me
the sun was actually the moon,
well, then my day
would turn to night.

Somehow, she always finds me,
Even though most days I can't find myself.
I'd rather be nowhere else,
no one else,
than the me I am
when I'm with her.

Filters

"Moving-in-day selfie!" she says
as she nudges into me
like that first day we met.

She pulls down her face mask
and smiles at me
through the filter of her phone,
a virtual layer of confidence.

"More like an 'ussie."
Now the green shirt
has words as he bombs
the screen's reflection
of our picture
in the phone.
Blasting the moment
that should be for us,

just Destiny
and me.
Something inside my chest
screeches to a halt.
It's like the sound waves
of his voice
cracked the windshield
of my heart.

"You're pretty when you smile," he says.

His arm reaches past me like
I'm not even there as his hand
cups hers and tilts the phone

in his direction.

Does he even see me?
He talks right through me.
Destiny gets that fidgety way

she gets when something's
out of place
or unexpected.
Like when a stone falls in pond
and the fish swim off
in all different directions,
but the fish are her thoughts.

"Thanks," she says
and pulls her hand away.
"Gotta get settled in."

"See you around," he says as if she
doesn't have a choice about it.

"Yeah...
Maybe."

The Dorm

She scans her new ID key card
on the contraption outside
the heavy side entrance door.
                              Up,

                      up,

                  up,

              up,

          up
six floors
of stairs that smell like
freshly cleaned institution.
Catching my breath in an attempt
to send oxygen to my burning thighs,
we stop as we pass
a warden disguised as a
hipster with a
WELCOMING DAY name tag:

                              Name: CAT
                    Pronouns: They/Them
                 Position: Resident Advisor

            "You're Destiny, right?" They ask.
              They must have met before.

      "Oh... yeah," she says.
      "And you're Cat, right? "

                              Cat taps their name tag
                    and grins an acknowledgement.
                    "Hey, we missed you just now
                          at the meeting where
                    we talk rules and expectations.
                              The biggest one,
                              we've got to log

all overnight visitations."
Cat nods in my direction.
"Just two per week, ok?
Wouldn't want anyone
just bunking up here.
You know?"

"Huh, thanks. I'll keep that in mind."

Destiny giggles like there would
never be a time that she would
sneak someone in.
But I'm not as cool about it.
How the hell do they know?
I've lived with ten different cats
over the course of my homes
but none that ever followed any rules.

"Oh, and quiet hours!"
Cat shouts to us down the hall.
"Keep it hushed
to a lull
after 10pm."

We turn the corner
to room 6314.
A red dot glows
through the tinted plastic
of the security camera dome.
Great. Just great.
Now there'll be footage, too.

Room 6314

                         "I'm going to have to get used
                              to all these keys."
                                  Giggling,
                                   fumbling,
                              she's not the best
                       at keeping track of things.

The door opens to a room
just big enough for a bed,
and a dresser,
and a desk.
                       "Isn't it awesome?" She sighs
                            then takes a deep breath
                              of independence,

as I breathe out hesitance.
I wish I could have
her faith in us
that this will all work out.
"Did you hear what Cat said?
How do they know?"

                         "Cat doesn't know.
                      That was a weird coincidence.
                              We'll be ok."

"How do you know?" I ask.

                              "I just know."

For the first time in hours
I take off my backpack
and I realize
it's holding everything I own.
Right there
on the floor

next to the
"Welcome to UVM" folder.
My whole world
fits in this 12'x12' room
that she's already decorated
with the finest
hand-me-down bedding
money can't buy.
Skeptically grateful, my eyes meet the hope in her eyes.

"We'll make it work," she says.

Sneaking

Sneaking out
and sneaking in,
how do I even begin
to make sense of all of this?
She picks up the folder
next to my bag
and hands me the brochure
for the cafeteria food plan.
Three meals a day
and extra spending for snacks,

> "Since when have we ever
> eaten three whole meals
> in one day?"

She has a point.
"And the bathroom?" I say.

> "That part's tricky,
> but I've figured it out.
> We'll both wear masks
> when we're out and about.
> Tie your hair back,
> like I showed you.
> Plus, really,
> who's going to
> look at you in the shower?"

"I can go there early,"

> "And I'll go late."

She snatches the brochure out of my hand
and points to the campus map on the back.

"Then there's bathrooms in all the buildings
to use the rest of the day."

"You really do have
this all figured out."

"I do."
She holds up two ID cards.

One from her freshman orientation,
hair tied back and masked,
One the way she looks today:
hair down, unmasked from 6 feet away.

"I told security I lost
the old one already."

I compare my face
in the mirror
to the face
on the card.

"They work.
I made sure."

Both her words
and her body
bounce on the bed
as visions of worries dance in my head.
But deep in my heart
I'm a survivor
and the only thing
I ever need
is love and trust.

A Destiny.

New People

There's a knock at the door.
I dive behind the pillows
on the bed,
so many pillows
for just one head.
That knock at the door?
It shouldn't be a surprise.
So many people
on just one floor.

"Hey! Destiny!
Y
o
u

i
n

t
h
e
r
e
?
It's Cat."
They call in from the hall.
"We're headed down to eat
before they close the cafe.
Wanna come with?"

"Uh, sure, just a minute!"
she calls back
grabbing her ID
and a face mask.
Then whispers to me

84

urgently,
"I have to live with them.
I think I should go.
I'll be back
with something for you to eat.
Please just stay here."

She says, "stay here,"
as if I have any where
else to go.

Hungry

There's a kind of hunger
no amount of ramen
will ever satisfy.
One that comes from
years of inconsistent meals.
Food is not a luxury
It's a necessity.
So, I'm really not all that picky.
I could never afford to be.

I never weigh myself
or count calories.
She knows I'll eat
whatever she brings back for me.

But there's a different kind of hunger
that craves connections.
That's where I'm selective.
I have aversions to
well,
most people.
If I let them in
it's all
or nothing.

Destiny has a sweet tooth for belonging.

And sometimes I hunger
for answers
like what will tomorrow look like?
I can't hide
in this room
forever.

Destiny has a sweet tooth for discovery.

And sometimes my hunger
longs for certainty.
There are hours
in the day
when my stomach aches
and my mind goes a little gray.
Losing control of the things I say,
my mood plummets.
I fade away.
Sometimes all I can do
is fall asleep
and hope when I wake
I'll feel better.

6

Destiny

Parallel Worlds

"What's your major?"
Cat asks as we follow the sidewalk
to the dining hall.
I'm not sure I would know my way
without them.

"Fishery and Wildlife."
My voice reeks
of imposter syndrome.
I've never been on
a boat before,
and I can hardly swim,
but something about
a quiet parallel world
where humans are the alien species
sounds like somewhere I'd like to be.
A place with no human feelings
and maybe the fish
won't notice if I panic.
"How about you?" I ask.

"Oh, I'm a third year
majoring in social work.
That's why I'm an RA,
to get experience helping people."

"That's cool,"
I say in a way
that gives away
that I don't really know
if I think it's cool.
"So, like, what do you want to do?
Work in child protection or something?"

Cat laughs.

"Why does everybody think that?
Nah, I think I want to work in a school."

"Oh, so am I giving you some
official student experience?"
Cat pauses as if they have to consider this.

"I guess, in a way.
But I would have invited you anyway."

Colors in the Cafe

Voices chatter
while trays clatter
on the counters of
so many lines.
So many choices.
So many voices.
So many people inside.
Thank goodness the chalkboard menus
are color coded:

Red – Today's Special – Chicken Lo Mein

Orange – A la Carte – sandwiches and wraps

Yellow – Soups

Green – there's no green.

I pat my pants pockets
front and back,
searching for my ID.
Just when I think I've lost it
it falls to the floor.
At his feet.
His shirt is green.

We both bend to pick up my Pegasus. He scoops it up.

Blue – his eyes waiting for me to say something.

Indigo – I learned my lesson about indigo
on the car ride here.
My crystal horse is latched to
my ID so I can carry my portable spectrums
with me.

Glancing down at the prism tilting
inconspicuously,
indigo and violet
complete the chain
and save me from the gray.

"You ok?" he asks.

My words come
slower than expected.
"Oh, yeah,
I'm sorry.
I'm just new.
Getting used to things here,"
I say as I reach
for my ID.

"You're the girl
from outside, right?
At the benches, earlier today?
I don't think I caught your name."

"I don't think I ever said."
He inspects my ID before
handing it back.

"Well, then,
here you go, Destiny.
Told you I'd see you again."

He keeps a hold on my crystal,
and for a moment we are
stuck like that together.

"So, you like horses?"

Pulling back, I stuff my ID and crystal
into the back pocket of my jeans.

"It's nothing,"
My heart races
as I try to catch my
breath in between beats.

"Ok, yeah." He steps back.
"Well, my name's Faris.
I'll see you around,
Destiny."

I want to rush after
him and tell
him that I'm not always
so awkward.
But that would probably
be awkward.

New Friends

Cat's got a spot
at a table in a corner
near the picture windows
looking out over the courtyard
of the buzzing campus.
Three familiar faces from our floor
in the dorm take
the empty seats near me.

"Ally,
Jess,
and Joanna," Cat points
to each of them.
"This is Destiny."

Scrunching my lips,
a nervous tic,
I give them a shy wave.

"Hi," says Joanna.

"What's up?" says Jess.

And Ally says, "Hey."

They talk so much
to each other that
I don't need to say a word.
There's a comfort in their noise,
their talk about nothing
that requires nothing
from me.

I have silence
in their chatter,

solace in their company.
And who I am is enough
just because
I am here
with them.

7

Brewen

Waking in a New Place
is jarring.
Somewhere in between
sleep and dying dreams
there's this place where my brain
finally finds true rest.
But when I wake
all that's real floods back
with waves of confusion,
doubt,
uncertainty.

A familiar shiver slinks up my spine
as my ears alert to every sound,
scan the shadows for any threats,
any hint of danger I may have missed,
hyper-vigilant,
ready for defense.
For a moment
my brain can't comprehend
where I am
or how I got here.
I jump at my silhouette
in the full-length mirror.
Can't make sense of the darkness
or the voices I hear
laughing in the hallway.

Until hers cuts through.

Her laugh, that is.
And I remember where I am,
where we are,
as the stale smell of dorm room
hits my nose
and the joy of her laugh
hits my heart.

Wherever she is
that's my home.

Maybe it's the sleep
or knowing that she's back
but somehow, I feel slightly better than before.
Better is a relative word
when it comes to my feelings.
When I say, "I feel better,"
it's better
than the shit I felt before
but ultimately, it's still
just slightly less shit.

Macaroni and Cheese (and a side of medication)

Of course, she brought me macaroni and cheese.
There're just some things that are always comforting,
And really, how can you screw up
Pasta
with butter
and cheese?

"Hey, Brew
I brought you
your food."
The crew down the hall is still commiserating.
"I can't believe I almost forgot about these."

Alprazolam

It's a wonder what
1.5 milligrams of the right medication can do
for her panic and anxiety,
her overall functioning.
It's like she's ready to handle anything.
Of course, it's doctor prescribed.
She's super careful about it,
we both are.
After what I have heard of
my mother's struggles with substances
there's no way I'm letting Destiny
take her chances
with addiction.
But this medication
lets her be more like her
and less like me.
For either of us
to be our best,
we both need her
to be her.

She raises it as if to toast,
"To our new place!"

We laugh like
she takes it for the both of us.
She pops the pill back
chasing it down
with the Pepsi
she brought me
from the cafeteria.

Then she plays her voicemail
on speaker phone.
"Destiny, Honey,

it's Ma.
We just got home.
Oh, and don't forget
to take your medication.
and drink lots of water."

The Acclimation Blues

Sometimes days fade
like a playlist on replay
into the background of your mind
and that's when you know things are getting
normal?
Comfortable?
Stable?

Some days disappear into routines.
Sometimes Destiny disappears
to her classes.

Monday - Wednesday – Friday.

She disappears to her work study
tracking invasive fish species
down by the lake.

Tuesday - Thursday.

Disappears to her meals
with the neighbors down the hall

breakfast - dinner.

Sometimes she just disappears.

I hardly see her anymore.

Muddy Waters

I apply for a job
at a coffee shop
On Main just off Church.
Not sure if it's named
after their coffee
or the lake,
but I like to think
it's for the amazing blues man,
who'd play guitar riffs in a creek
when he was a boy.
Either way
at Muddy Waters
there is coffee
and music
and ambiance.

All the boxes on the application
ask for something simple
just one tiny check.
But the answers aren't simple,
they're something more complex.
Asking my demographics like:
What's my culture?
My race? My sex?
All these ways to try to quantify
my human experience.
Where is the box to check
that I was a foster?
How is this any judge of my character?
When I hand it to the manager
                              he says, "These are mostly blank."
"Yeah," I say,
"I don't understand what
any of those questions have to do with
how I work with people,

104

or how I make coffee.
I don't have the answer for many of them anyway.
I'm still figuring out who I am."

"You can make a decent coffee?" he asks.

"I can definitely follow a recipe."

"Can you start on Tuesday?"

I had to use
Destiny's ID
and number for social security
to become an official employee.
So, I am Destiny on paper.
But officially unofficially
my name tag says Brewen.
It's the only place
I can be me,
not hidden away.

COVID-19 guidelines for staff
require masks
and I am grateful
for the simple barrier
between me and the world.
Most days I disappear to cover shifts.
But there's a quiet sadness growing
between us
as Destiny and I
drift.

The Homework/ Home/Work Balance

She's balancing an open book on her lap
and about 50 tabs
shifting on her screen.
Destiny's working on her lab
for microbiology
while she waits for the timer to go off
to switch our laundry
in the washing machines down the hall.
I try to keep quiet so she can concentrate
on the balance of life
for the fish on the lake.
But she's so geeked out
she can't help but share.
Eyes still focused on her screen,
she talks to me through the
computer glare.

"Isn't it amazing how ecosystems work?
Each form of life
has their worth,
an interdependence,
a balance,
a give and take that contributes
to the health and sustainability of all."

Just then the timer buzzes for the laundry.

"Oh no, is it seriously already 2:30
a.m.?
I still have so much to do
before my morning class."

"What time's that at?"
I ask.

She says, "10."

"I can get the laundry,"
I say, reaching for my mask.
"Everyone else is already asleep.
Nobody will see me.
I'll be right back."

And when I return with the hamper
of freshly folded clothes
she's already
fallen asleep.
I set her alarm for 6am
to give her time to finish up her lab
before she has to leave.

Balance is a moving target.
Why didn't anyone ever say
this independence thing
would be so much work?
So little sleep.
So many things to keep
track of.
So much laundry.

8

Destiny

Lab Partners

It's 9:45am when I hit submit
on my microbiology lab.
That leaves me 10 minutes
to get to class.
I guess I'll be wearing yesterday's clothes.
Good thing I only have this course
every
other
day.

"Alright class," says Professor Thomsen,
"We'll try partners for labs today."

So, everyone looks around,
taking in the silent messages
from each other's eyes.
I adjust the nose wire of
my face mask. Tug at the straps
that suddenly feel tight
behind my ears.
My brain fills in
other people's facial features.
The ones I can't see.
A smile.
Full cheeks.
A dimple.
The guy behind me, his eyes
seem to see right through me.
Picking partners
in a sea of partial faces
raises my anxiety.
I work my way through rainbows
and find my familiar green
shirted friend,
with the blue in his eyes.

Flipping my keychain in my hands,
the indigo and violet
glint back at me.
So much
smoother
than before.

"See, I told you I'd see you around," Faris says.

"You need a partner?" I ask.

"Depends.
Well, I mean, I'm a Poli – Sci major,
microbiology really isn't my thing.
So, you'd have to, you know,
be the one doing most of it.
How good are you at labs?
Like you'll write this up for me?"

"Uh ...
Yeah.
I mean,
I guess
that works."
If he lets me
do all the work
at least we won't have
a chance to disagree.
And maybe he'll see
I'm not just some flake
who sometimes forgets how to speak.

Ode to Rainbow Smelt and Data Collection

The thing about fish
is they don't judge my anxiety,
or talk like I'm not there.
This is why field study
is so much better than labs.
The research boat bounces
to the middle of Lake Champlain
to collect data on
the fish populations
in its largest basin.
There's a whole world
beneath the water's surface
that knows nothing about me.
I'm the alien here,
the visiting life form.
It feels good to be
unknown.

Hydro-acoustic sonar
bounces sound against life
transposing acoustics
to color-coded graphs
for visual inspection.
Each color represents
a different species.
Red – Orange – Yellow – Green – Blue – Indigo - Violet
Trout,
alewife,
mysis,
and my new favorite,
rainbow smelt.

Like a school of fish
the crew onboard
move together

trawling nets,
catching,
counting,
inspecting,
documenting,
and releasing,
bouncing
me from the nets
I've caught myself inside.

Swimming Rainbows

I measure a six-incher
against a yard stick.
Its mottled scales glimmer in the sun.
Eyes wide, intent on me,
it looks like it's pleading to survive
this alien encounter.

"Don't worry, little rainbow,"
I say as if it understands.
"We are all just trying to help."

Once all the fish are clipped
we release them
back into their home.
It's almost as if they don't
recognize they're safe
as they pause in shock
before they swim away.

I never knew rainbows could swim.

A Few Notes on:

Energetic Pathways
shared in ecosystems,
each organism
holds its own potential,
each dependent on the others
directly
and
indirectly.

Some ecosystems are
more vulnerable
to invasion.

Some ecosystems thrive
despite invasion.

Energetic pathways balance life
between the invasive and non-invasive species.

Factors to consider:
habitat availability
levels of nutrients
hypoxicity
(because even fish need to breathe.)

9

Brewen

Sounds in the Coffee Shop

The clamor of dishes,
the hiss of steam,
the silent pauses
and the laughs that crescendo
and fall in between.
Ambient noise
about 70 decibels or so
is scientifically known
to boost human neurological capacities.
It's my soothing social blanket
the hum of voices
that aren't talking directly to me.
Their words, indecipherable,
but their presence is comforting.

Kyler is the shift manager
training me.
He floats on the noise
as if it's a cloud of vibrations
of his own energy.
Ambient.
Comforting.
Gliding from the register to the refrigerator
adding ice to the machine,
pouring coffee into the blender,
moving through the world intentionally.
His is the only voice
in all this noise
that I have to understand.

                                      "So, we call you Brewen?" he asks.

"Yeah, and as you say it out loud
I am just now noticing the irony."

"Irony?" He says.

"Like I'm Brewen coffee?"
Even his laugh is unassuming,
It bubbles up quietly like
the froth in a latte.

"I didn't think of that.
But now that you mention it..."

"Please, forget that I mentioned it."

"Forgotten.
Actually, I was thinking....
Aren't you in class with me?"

"Class?" I ask.

"Yeah, Intro to Marine Biology.
I sit two rows behind...
I think her name is Destiny.
Isn't your real name Destiny?
Is that you?"

"Oh, Biology?
Destiny?
That's interesting.
Another girl who looks like me
and has the same name?"
I jiggle and turn
the glass pot to
try to fit it in the machine.
Fumbling,
I almost drop it
but Kyler intervenes.
For a moment we both
have our hands on the pot.
Our eyes lock.

My heart stops.

"No, That's not me.
I go by Brewen."
He looks at me
almost skeptically
as if he can't believe his eyes
but he appears to want
to believe me.

                                        "Yeah, I guess it's a big place."

As he shows me
all the drink recipes
and substitutions
I can't help but remember
that feeling on the field trip
when Destiny fell into my lap
as Kyler's hips nudge mine ever so slightly
to make room for both of us
in front of the machines.
And I can't help but smile
as my heart makes room for him, too.

V   for Victorious

The buzz of the coffee shop
seems to pause
as an older man enters the door.

                                        "One small,
                                           hot
                                         coffee,
                                          black
                                        please,"
                                        he says.

"I can handle that," I say as I pour
a cup of our finest brew.

                                  "You're new here."
                                     He notices.

Maybe it's the way I fumble
with even the smallest orders.
"Is it that obvious?" I ask.
Hoping he can see hints
of my nose scrunching
behind my mask.

                "You are new like a breath of fresh air.
                                           While me?
                              Well, I'm experienced here."
                                 He leans in and whispers
                            as if just the two of us will hear,
                          "You see, I like to say experienced
                                         instead of old."

"Kind of like that experienced juke box over there?
Loved for a long time
and you know all the best songs?"

121

"See, I knew I liked you."
He bounces his pointer finger at me
while the other four secure his cup.
"Are you really Brewen?"
His laugh emphasizes
his sarcasm
with a booming, "HA! HA!"

"Am I really...?
Oh, like the coffee?
Well, yeah, I guess I am."

"Nice to meet you, Brewen."
He spreads his arms wide
like a boxer who's just won a fight.
"I'm V.
for Victorious
because this is the life
I will win."

There is something about this man's soul
that is familiar
like maybe we've walked down this road
together before.

"Do you play chess at all, Brewen?"
He pats his messenger bag
and it rattles like it's got
fragments of the world inside.

"Actually,
I do.
I mean sometimes."
My arms press against the counter
like I'm getting psyched up
to take on this world champion.
Push, press, push, press.

"Well, we'll have to play sometime.
And I'll win that, too."

"I bet you will, Mr. V. for Victorious."

Chess

For the rest of my shift my thoughts drift
to games with Jandro
and even further back
to therapy sessions
in fifth grade.
The counselor would come to my school
because that was the only place
in my life that was quiet.
But I was always quiet.
Sometimes silent.
Sometimes silent for years.

I didn't trust most people
and I didn't trust most words.
Not mine.
Not theirs.
So, this counselor,
she got that she couldn't make me talk.
But there were things she could teach me.
There were ways she reached me.
The one I remember most
was chess.
All those little pieces laid out there on the board.
Organized.
Predictable.
Like a little world
where I was in control,
of my pieces, anyway.

"This will help you with strategy," she said.
"How to think futuristically,
You have to predict the moves
that your opponents will make,
the turns you want to take.
And every game you'll see you will improve."

124

And she was right.
I did improve.
In more ways than chess moves.
We would laugh.
Then we would talk.
And my trust in myself
and the world
got a little stronger every time.

Was that why Jandro always brought his board?

A Game with V

Most days when my shift lets out
I walk to the waterfront
down the path
dodging bicyclists
and dedicated walkers
in coordinated athleisure wear,

past the docks
with eclectic groups
of sunset watchers
writing, arting, dreaming,

beyond the skatepark
where skaters pause time
as they trick mid-air
and land safely
on boards
in constant motion,
befriending physics
and gravity,

to the quieter parts
along the shore
where there's just
sand, the
water,
and me.

Today the water makes me feel small
in a good way.
Like whatever choices I make,
good or bad,
are insignificant
compared to vastness of the universe.
As I head back

a voice calls for me,
and I know who it is before I see
by the clever lilt in his voice.

"Just in time!
I saved you a seat."

V. pushes the chair out
from the other side of a portable card table
with his feet.
I look down at my watch to check the time.

"Oh seriously?" he says.
"Where do you have to be right now?
You promised me a game."

"I was just checking.
There's someone expecting me.
But I can stay for
just one game."

"You just have to play until I win."
He winks with years behind his confidence.

"Well, that sounds like you think
it won't take long."
My left eyebrow raises to counter his grin.
His board is all tattered and torn,
like it's been places.
His hands gently reflect
his strategic thoughts
as they hover over the pieces.

Twenty-five moves in, he says.
"I thought I'd have had you by now."
His finger taps the crown of his queen.
"You play like someone who's had experiences."

"I told you I played a little chess."

"Not just chess,
I mean life experience.
You play like you have a history
of strategic thinking."

This would usually be when
I'd get up and never talk to someone again.
Who is he to think he
can see right through me?
But part of me wonders if he can.
And another part of me wants
to trust and talk with someone again.
"I don't really know my history," I say.

"Well, wherever,
whatever you came from
it's clear to me
that you're right here
right now
and you may be one of the only people
to have ever beat me."

"You're in check," I say
as my rook clears his line of pawns.

"See, I knew that was coming."

"But all you have to do is move your Queen."

"Maybe I shouldn't tell you this,
but as much as I like to win.
I never,
I mean not ever,
sacrifice my queen."

I feel kind of guilty
when I take his king.

"I knew you'd be
a worthy adversary.
Until next time, my friend."

"Yes, we will have to play again."

"I told you; we play until I win.
I didn't say it had to be today."

Pawn and King

When I return to the dorm
the sky is a purple mid-September sunset
glowing off the lake.
The two reflect each other
as if they are the same
with no defining line
where the sky ends
and the lake begins.

No one notices me
when I use our extra key
to swipe my way in.
If I enter the dorm
while most of the floor
is still at dinner,
I can disappear into her room
undetected.

I leave my first paycheck
on her desk.
It's written in her name.
Placing it where I know she'll see it
next to her boxed-up chess set
she brought for us
to play together.
But we never have time to play
or really just be
together.

If this world is a game
it's clear that I am a pawn,
plotting hard on the defense
to make sure
my king survives.

I have one move.
I can only move forward.

I keep my pocket full of tips
because sometimes
even a pawn needs
some control of the board.

Cat, A Tonic

My stomach gurgles a reminder
that I haven't eaten
since yesterday.
The floor is so quiet
I figure it might be safe
to chance the three minutes
to microwave
some ramen.
I put my mask on just in case.
For two and a half minutes
I was right.
It was clear
until...

                    "Oh, hey! I thought I was the only one here."

With no time to see which way Cat jumps,
I bound to face the microwave
as they approach.
The threat of flashbacks,
of sirens and fire,
crouches in the atmosphere
ready to pounce me
and entrance me
into the fog of my reactivity.
But I manage to stave it off
disguised by this mask that clings to me
and conceals
the details of my face.
"So did I," I say
and focus my gaze on the microwave

35...34...33.

Somehow the countdown comforts me

as my panic stands by
still
ready to pounce.

"Didn't everybody head off to the show?"
Cat reaches into the refrigerator
and pops open a tonic water.

"The show?"

"That comedian at The Flynn."

"Oh, yeah. I told them to go ahead without me."

"Yeah, not my thing either."

"Yeah." An awkward pause
I can't fill
magnifies the hum
of the microwave.
At least it masks the sound
of the beating
of my tell-tale heart.

"Is everything ok?"

21... 20... 19...

"Uh, yeah. I just have to work early on Saturdays."

"I didn't realize they still count fish on Saturdays."

16... 15... 14...

Oh no, I hope my cover's not blown.
Why do some seconds take so long
especially when you're waiting
for them to move on?

If Cat wasn't the one who
could expel me to the street
I think they could be my friend.
So kind,
like the kind that lets you know
you're not alone
and would follow you to the end.
But I still have to pretend.
I can't let this Cat's eyes
see into my soul
or else they'll know
and that would mean defeat
for Destiny and me
and them.

9... 8... 7...

"Are you sure you're ok?
You don't seem like yourself today."

5... 4... 3...

"Yeah, I think I'm just tired." I say.

2... 1.
Beep, beep, beep.
goes the microwave.

"I think I just need to eat
and get a little sleep."

I'm pretty sure Cat's eyes see right through me.

10

Destiny

Zone of Repulsion

Church street
has its very own
energetic pathways.
Life flowing
through vegan restaurants
across from breweries
serving steaks.
Drummers circle
thumping rhythms
into clouds of marijuana smoke.

Even the air dances.

Different folks emerge for the nightlife
than the business people
and shoppers
around in the day.
But day and night
the cobblestones
are still the same
as they were a hundred years ago.

Day or night,
this place feels safe.

Jess is all excited about this
comedian at the Flynn.
The show starts at 8,
and it's 7:37.
They just finished dinner
when I catch up with them.

"I hope there's tickets left," Jess says
as she walks ahead.
Her dressy boots clip – clop – clip

on the cobblestones.

Fish swim in schools,
each independent beings
swimming together
for a common purpose
and protection.

Ally, Joanna, and I
are like a silent school
veering this way and that
mindlessly following Jess.

When we pass by Muddy Waters,
I take my time to peek inside.
I know Brewen's not at work,
but there's this guy
stacking chairs
to close up
for the night.

He must see me looking
because he waves.
He seems nice.
I wonder
if Brewen
ever works
with him?

Noticing the disruption
of my attention
to the lateral line movements
of my school of friends,
I trip
and fall into a different him.

"You're lucky I need you
for our lab report," Faris says

                                    as he pulls me up to stand.

I wipe away the dust
and check the damage
to my legs.
The guy in the coffee shop window
sees Faris
and fades away.
"Sorry about that," I say.

                              "Where are you headed?" he asks.

"Oh, uh..."
All my thoughts scatter
like fish that don't want
to be caught.

                              Ally circles back and links arms
                                    with me, "We're headed
                                          to the Flynn."

She pulls me forward to
catch up with Joanna and Jess
like our shoal has lost the rest of the school.
Ally minds my zone of repulsion,
the space a fish maintains
as not to collide
with its neighbors.

Shoaling

A 1930s art deco sign
greets the four of us
outside the Flynn Theatre.
We raise our masks up
to approach the ticket window.

The woman tells us,
"There's just three seats left.
$63 each."

And that's ok because
that kind of money
is a lot for me.
"You all should go," I say.
"I can make it back on my own."

"Seriously, we don't have to go," says Jess.
"Yeah," says Ally, "We don't
want to leave you on your own."

But they all already have
their cards out to pay.

"No, really, I'll
catch you after.
Seriously.
I will be ok."

"Ok, but we hate going without you."
"But we better go."
"We're already late."

They swim off together
into a sea of other fish
while I shoal off alone.

Free Trade

There are so many people
on the streets
laughing,
playing music,
conversating,
vibing with each other's energy.
Even though I'm on my own
I feel like I'm in good company.

Some of the stores are still lit up,
open for the evening crowd.
Novelties in the free trade store
window display
catch my eye.

The sign on the door says:
DEAR CUSTOMERS,
PLEASE WEAR MASKS.
I pull mine up and step inside.

Customers buzz as they root through treasures,
singing bowls and handmade candle holders,
the smell of incense and essential oils,
massage rocks and crystals,
wooden drums from India,
metal art from Haiti...

A quartz chess board from Pakistan
draws me in.
Each piece is slightly different
in its handmade elegance.
I check the price
and suddenly feel unworthy
of even handling
the queen in my hand.

$150 out of my price range
but a price more than fitting
for the amount of time and skill
someone from another side of the world
devoted to it.

"Do you play?" A man asks
as he sifts through a basket
of odds and ends.

There's something about this man's soul
that is familiar
like maybe we've walked down this road
together before.
"Sometimes," I say.
"I just play sometimes with a friend."

"That's a beautiful set," he says.

"It definitely is.
But it's way too much for me."

"Is it missing a piece?" he asks.

I check:
queens, kings, horsemen, rooks,
bishops,
and fifteen pawns.
"Looks like it's missing a pawn."

"Well, that's a shame," he says.
"I wonder if
it got mixed in here.
Sorting through stone, wood,
and fabric figures, his eyes
brighten when he finds,
"Not an exact match,"
he holds up a crystal pawn,

"but she can play for either side."
The crystal catches the light
splashing bursts of color
onto the board.

Red- orange – yellow – green – blue – indigo – violet.
"It's beautiful," I say.

"How about a game?"

"Right here in the store?"

"Sure thing," he says.
"The manager won't mind."
He taps the name tag
on his worn button up shirt.

VICTORIOUS
Store Manager
10,000 Villages

Victorious

The manager reaches out to place the pawn
into starting position.
Suddenly Faris moves in
from the side.
He grabs the pawn from the old man's hands.

"Alright, alright," Faris says.
"That's enough, old man.
She's not playing any games tonight.
Why would she stay here
and play chess with you,
when she could go
to the club with me?"

My heart skips
enough beats
for ten thousand villages.
Where did those spectrums go?
While I search for red,
I see it rise in the old man's eyes.

"Perhaps you should let
the young lady
speak for herself."

But I'm at a loss for words
as the world
loses its colors.
Faris takes my arm
and pulls me from the store.
Orange – I can't find orange
as my eyes adjust to the night.

"I thought you went to that show
with your friends?" he says.

My words are locked in tight.

"Anyway, I'm glad I saw you." He laughs.
"That guy was such a creep.
Here, I got you this."
He hands me the crystal pawn.

I shift it to the light,
its spectrums saving me
from the gray.
"But you didn't pay for this,"
I say when my words return.

"Consider it a complimentary gift
for your troubles?"

"I don't think
I was in any trouble," I say
and back away,
into the door we just
came out of.

The old man has moved on
to another part of the store,
but I see his eyes peek up
when I place the pawn
back into the basket she came from.
He chuckles to himself,
the laugh of a small victory.

Should I apologize?
But I can see Faris still waiting outside,
and I don't want to reenact that last scene.
So, I head out the door
to find out what the rest of the night
has in store for me.

Nobody's Perfect

So, maybe Faris had it wrong
what that old man was all about,
but really, he cared enough about me
to step in.
Nobody's perfect.
Not all the time.
Especially not me.
Especially not to me.

I kind of like that he notices me
even from far away
and he seems to accept
the times I can't talk
when my mind starts to turn gray.
He takes me to a brewery
where we hang outside
lost in a crowd
drinking beers.
He buys.

I'm not a big drinker.
I really shouldn't be
drinking anything.
The effects of beer + alprazolam
don't really agree
with my mind
or my stomach.

"Don't forget to take your meds,"
Ma's text
hits my phone
right at that moment
and reminds me
that I did
forget.

The way I figure it,
drinking will have
less side effects
on a night like this.

"So, what's up with how
sometimes you seem like
you're in a different place?
Like when you get all spacey?"

"You'd think it was weird
if I told you," I say.

"I will think it's more weird
if you don't."

"I don't know how to explain
it exactly.
My old therapist said it had
something to do with panic
mixed with OCD.
Like I start to freeze
and the only thing that stops me
from all out dissociation
is...
never mind.
It's stupid really."

"Seriously," he says.
"You can tell me."

"The only thing that saves me
is finding all of the colors
of the rainbow
in order."

"Ok," he says

in a way that makes me feel
both accepted
and crazy.
"That's specific," he laughs.

"See?!
I knew I shouldn't have
said anything."

"No, really," he says.
"I think it's cute.
Rainbow colors...
I bet you likes them Lucky Charms!"
He dances like a
foolish Leprechaun.

I put my drink
down on the bar
and turn to walk away.

"C'mon," he says
as he grabs my arm.
"I was just kidding.
Thought I'd lighten it up a bit.
How often does it happen?"

"Sometimes every day.
Sometimes not for weeks."

"Is that why you have
that little horse on your keys."

Feeling vulnerable
I nod.
No one has ever known
about my keychain,
not since the teacher
who gave it to me.

Not
even
Brewen.

"So, what happens if you
don't see your rainbow?"
He seems genuinely interested.

"I just turn off.
Like something
or someone else
is at the controls
and my body's frozen
until I wake up."

"Yikes." He holds up his beer.
"Well, let's say a toast,
to not losing your shit tonight!
Let's have some fun!" He yells.

And somehow,
someway,
sharing my imperfections
helps me put them aside
and they don't dominate
my time with him anymore.

We have a night unlike any I've ever had before.

11

Brewen

Destiny Returns

She's laughter for days when
she bursts in the door
unquietly
like maybe she means to wake me.
Suddenly the room is bright.
Light beams from the ceiling
off the mirror
into my eyes.
"What time is it?"
I wince at the sour light,
and her sour breath
leaves a bad taste in my mouth.

"2 a.m.,
but I have to tell you
about..."
She pulls out her phone and scrolls to
a picture of . . .
"him."

The green shirt.
Groan.

"Oh, I'm sorry about the light."

But it's not the light.
I don't tell her the groan's for him.
She goes on to explain
how she saw him
in the cafeteria
and again,
in biology class.
His name
is Faris.
So I ask,

152

"Like the wheel?"

She's slightly annoyed.
"No. Like F-A-R-I-S."

But I'm more than slightly annoyed.

"Why can't you just be happy for me?"
And now I'm feeling slightly destroyed
by the tinge of anger in her voice.

"I'm always happy for you,"
I say, masking my frustration
about this situation
about the green shirt.
I want to say,
Does he always wear a green shirt?
But instead I say,
"I just miss you."

Her body shifts from tense to relaxed.
"I miss you, too.
We've both got so much we have to do
creating a life for ourself.
But hey,
I got invited to a party tomorrow.
You should come, too."

"What about your friends down the hall?"

"I thought it could be
just you and me
and, you know,
whoever shows up to this off-campus thing."

And I think I know
who "you know" and "whoever" means.
As much as I'd rather not test

how I will react around him
I need some time with her again.

Just to feel whole.

Feelings

I don't feel things like other people do.
Take joy, for example.
Joy, pure joy,
like excited skipping,
handholding,
cartwheeling joy...
yeah, that doesn't happen for me.
When life is a montage of moments of survival,
joy, for me
is in the moments
in between.

Gina used to be joyful
on those days between
Thanksgiving and Christmas
but not on the actual holidays.
Those days held too much stress
and expectations.
But the days in between,
those days were the best.
Full of songs and love and light.

My joy
is in the steps between raindrops,
the rays that break through the clouds,
the pause between heartbeats,
the rests between sounds.

The conversations between classes.
Temps between 68 and 74.
When I'm almost to, "I've got this,"
when I've never done this before.

In the moments between meals
when the next one is not on my mind,

the space on the paper where my words
dance on the lines.

My joy is simple.
It's not an event.
It's a thread
binding me together
weaving through the in between.

Like the time between an invite
and the actual party,
full of excitement and anticipation,
and I haven't been let down yet.

Party Games

Music blaring.
People staring.
Is it my mask?
Or the outfit I'm wearing?
Either way I'm not caring
for this buzzing crowd tonight.

Drinking.
Thinking.
Strobe lights blinking.
This frat house stinking.
We find a spot outside.
On the patio
where the ratio
of space to people
is enough for me to catch my breath.

"Hey, let's play chess,
there's a board," Destiny says
as she checks herself
in the reflection of the glass French doors.

I nod a yes
because this might be my only chance
for it to be just us tonight.
She's watching people through the door
like she's waiting for something more,
some kind of cure
to take her to her own destiny.
And I feel in my heart
that it's not enough for her tonight
that she's sharing this space with me.

Sitting,
waiting,

conversating
on love and mating,
this game we're playing,
Should she play loud or soft?

Faris makes his way outside
and catches her eye.
It's like he knows she's
incomplete,
like he can sense
what makes her weak.

Pawn and Knight and King

If Destiny's the king,
and I'm a pawn,
then Faris is a knight,
playing against me.
He's not on our team.

They talk a while.
She likes his style.
He makes her smile.
This goes on and on all night.

Faris= Horseman = Knight

I don't know exactly why
I don't like him.
Maybe it's the way he looks at her
like he thinks he knows her
but he talks to her
like she's not as smart as she is.

Maybe it's the way she doesn't seem to mind.
Maybe it's the way he watches other girls
when she looks away from him.
Maybe it's the way he gets too close.

Or maybe, it's the way she looks at him
instead of me
and laughs at his stupid jokes,
the ones I know she doesn't think are funny.

Maybe it's because she seems like someone else,
someone less than she actually is,
when she's with him.
Maybe it's the way he looks right through me
as if I don't exist.

I think this knight is the horseman
of my personal apocalypse,
but I'm not sure which one.
Is he conquest, war, famine, or death?

Maybe it's something else.
Maybe it's all of this.

12

Destiny

Before Last Night

the thought had never crossed my mind
that there would be a guy
I'd meet
so serendipitously
and he would
accept me for
who I am.
He looks at me
like he thinks I'm fun
or maybe
it's interesting.
I've never been near a guy
so intent on
looking out for me.

Before last night
I'd never really had
so much as one whole drink.
But nothing went wrong last night
so, I'm pretty sure
tonight will be the same.

Before last night
I hadn't really considered
what a second date might mean
until he leans in to kiss me
and I see rainbows
in my mind.

Pour Me

another drink,
I think I might be on four.
Brewen's probably counting
for me.
She's always so careful
for me.
Tonight, I wish she would just
lighten up.
Enjoy herself
for me.

But instead, she's all like,
"Poor me."
Watching the door hyper-vigilantly
like there's some danger
seeking its opportunity.

But I am here with Faris.
Safe to let my guard down.
I even laugh when he takes
my horse charm off my keys
and says,

"You don't need this anymore.
You've got me."

My little Pegasus
flies from his hand
into the bushes.

13

Brewen

The Rook

Sometimes when you're in the middle of a game
you forget there are different pieces,
forget how they move,
and how they will affect you.
They approach you unexpectedly
like how Kyler zooms a straight line toward me.

                    "I didn't know you'd be here," he says.

"Me either," I say
keeping my eye on the green knight
because if I lose track of him
he might win.

                "The party just got that much better," he says.

And usually, I'd agree.
But right now, I can't let him distract me.
"I'm here with a friend," I say.
He follows the line of my attention
to the target of my contention.

                            "Oh, right, ok," he says
                                as he moves away.

"Oh! No!
It's not like that."
I try to explain.
But he's already gone.

Rooks need open lines on the board
to move back and forth,
to increase their importance,
and meet their potential.
My heart sinks

because I think I just cut Kyler off.

I hope he's still in play.

Zugzwang

Sometimes any possible move
will threaten your position.
You still have to move.
Make a decision.

Knights on the Board

move their best in a crowd
where they use distractions to advance their position
while the other pieces are vulnerable
trapped in cluttered spaces.

Fork tricking,
slyly moving,
advantage improving,
he slips something in her drink.
He must think
I don't see his moves,
but I see right through
his deception.
My interception of her drink
is more than slightly less effective
than I intended
as it pours onto her lap.
I reach to help her,
but she pushes me back
and says,

"Why are you ruining everything?"

Doesn't she know what I know?
Can't she see what I see?
I guess that if she can't
I'd rather have her mad at me
than drugged up by this dude.
She's too drunk to care.
He walks her home.
It's like I'm not there.
But I won't let go.
I follow them both.
She'll hate me, I know,
but I can't let him do

what I think he might do
up in the room.

14

Destiny

Slip to the Gray

The difference in me
after a couple of drinks
is that I don't even notice
the signs
that I'm slipping
from
my
own
mind.

No
time
for
rainbows.

I just
want
to

close

my

eyes.

15

Brewen

Knights on the Board– II

She's stuck inside
all these lies
and all that she can't leave behind.
A far-off stare,
her shoulders bare,
I know that she's not there,
not inside those eyes.

She's stepped out of her soul.
She's stepped out of her brain.
Something in those drugs has
crossed her membranes.

The green knight's a predator,
a kind she's never known before.

So, I step in for her.

Gambit

From the start of the game
a pawn knows there's a chance
that she will have to be sacrificed
to protect the king.

My King's in Check

I only get one move,
one moment
until his green shirt is on the floor.
The blaring sound in my ears rings
before I'm completely unaware
of how we get from
that moment

.

.

.

to this moment
like we've skipped three steps.
And when I come back to,
he grabs his green shirt
and the bottle of Destiny's meds
as he flees out the door.
Cat's shadow in the hallway light peeks inside.
I hear them ask us through the dark,

"Hey, is everything ok?"

My neck forces my head to nod,
as I create a barrier with my arms
to protect the shell that's left of me.

Then Cat calls toward where Faris fled
in their assertive protective way,
"You are not authorized to be here. I'll show you out."
But he's already got away.

The room looks like a bomb went off.
It's me.
I'm that bomb again,
I'm sure.

I sit outside myself,
watching me,
watching her
through the reflection
of the mirror
I don't remember
breaking.
The air is heavy
like a sweaty green shirt tossed on the floor.
Destiny rests quietly.
I don't think she'll want me here anymore.

When She Wakes

she covers her ears and winces
at the light
on the ceiling.
Outside it's still dark.
Still night.

"It's all out of tune," she says. "My life,
no matter how high I go.
There's always some sort of discord.
What happened here?
Where'd he go?"

I open my mouth
but the words don't come out.
Where do I start to explain?
I don't want to add to the dissonance.
Don't want to add to her pain.
But she must sense my overwhelm
and see the room turned upside down,
the cracked mirror on the floor.

"Brew, you did it again?"

"Well, no,
but yes,
but no..."
Our eyes reflect
an infinite
picture in a picture
in a picture
in the schism of
the looking glass.
It's not shattered
just cracked.
I try my best to

178

hang it
back where it belongs.

                    "Brew, I think
                    you have to go."

She doesn't understand
I was trying to protect her.
"But Destiny, he's just no good – "

                    "Brew, you've ruined everything!
                         You need to go!"
              Her whole body shakes through angry tears.

Does she think it was me
or maybe my jealousy
who was out to get her?
This isn't the moment to explain.
She's not ready.
She won't hear me.
And honestly,
isn't she better off without me?
Maybe I do ruin everything.

Out of Play

My life in one bag over my shoulder,
I head down the hall
on autopilot,
no destination anymore.
Nowhere to be.
Nowhere to stay.
Nowhere to call home.
This goodbye is no good.
It's just bye.
And it's never hurt like this before,
because I'm no good, not even for her.
I left my heart in room 6314.

"Where are you going? Are you ok?"
Cat spreads their arms to take up space
blocking my way through.

I turn my maskless face away,
"I'm fine. Please,
just let me get by."

"Do you want to talk about
what happened back there?
What did he do to you?"

"I'm really not ready for any kind of talk.
But thanks.
Maybe another time.
I think I just need to walk."

"Ok. I'll stop by tomorrow.
Please be safe out there.
You know where I am
if you need me."

Just when I think there is no one

in this world who cares
there is someone out there who shows up
to help when I least expect it.
Someday I will have to figure out
how to let myself
accept it.
But if Cat figures out
I've been living here,
Destiny could lose
her scholarship,
and she doesn't need
to lose anything else tonight.

Change

I don't know about change if I can handle this.
I don't know about faith if I can manage it.
I don't know about life if I can get through this.
I don't know about love when I'm missing it.
I try to love
I try to work
I try to live
I try to make a place where I'll fit in.
But all these changes
they filter through
and when it comes down to it
I have to accept that you
can't have me here anymore.
So where do I go now?
What do I do
when I built myself around you?

Latitude and Longitude

The human mind
tries to organize
the world in neat little boxes,
straight lines that intersect
at perpendicular angles,
X axis
and Y.
Vertical.
Horizontal.
Rank and file,
Dark and light.
Latitude and longitude.
But I don't fit into a box,
none of us really do.

I have to escape this grid of streets
North, south, east, west.
Coordinated intervals of traffic lights
tell me when to walk.
If only I had a traffic light in my brain
that could tell me when to stop.
Maybe then I could stay safe.
For me.
For everyone else.

All these things we organize
in our attempt to control
all the things that are out of our control.

Hands on a clock
go in one direction.
Always forward.
Never back.
They map out our days
without pausing to make sure

we're keeping up
with our self-imposed sense of urgency.
We scribble our days into calendars,
mark checks on lists
get lost in the hustle
until we wonder where time went
because we lost track of it
while we were so busy
keeping track of it.

Walking along the path by the water
I follow the light of the moon in the sky.
There are no bikes at night.
Well, at least, not tonight.
The moon leads me to
a circle of stones
like an ancient henge on the shore.
Standing in the center
I cast no shadow
on this earth clock.
If I can't measure time here at night
does it even really pass?
The stars in the sky move
the same ways they always have
since before the concept of time.

Ancient people mapped stars in constellations
in an attempt to leave
the stories of their souls
written in the sky
echoing back so many years later
in the language of light.
Whispering,
"Don't forget I was here."

Maybe someday people will learn
how to map our hearts
measure our feelings

weigh our worth.

The Stars

stand by quietly
withholding the words of wishes
tossed to them
from thousands of years
of souls
who stood on these shores
searching for answers.
I wish I could reach out to touch them
as if maybe
they could heal me.

The lake water laps at my feet
tapping my toes
calling my attention.
This same water has shared time
absorbing,
reflecting,
refracting their light
for as long as there has been water,
as long as there has been night.
These illuminated strangers
don't seem so out of reach
mirrored in the water
where my reflection is just a contour
floating on the surface.
I reach out to the shadow girl
reaching out to me.

The thing about water
is that no matter how vast
or how deep,
it redistributes weight.
I could float on top,
starfishing,
or dive under

into the deep.
But however deep I go
the water will not crush me
because I know how to swim.
But it threatens to drown me
if I spend too much time holding
my breath.

As I touch the silhouette
against the backdrop of stars
the water ripples
and her hand disappears into mine.
We are one.
I am the girl in the shadow,
spangled in starlight.
I borrow her ability to not feel
as the water redistributes
the weight in my heart.

There are so many things I need to figure out.
But this moment
to the next
is the only one
I have to handle
right now.

16

Destiny

The Looking Glass

is cracked in
a clean schism
of two halves
that make a whole.
It mirrors me like
there are endless possibilities.
An infinite number of me
divide
through space and time
like the colors that split
inside a rainbow
that are really
only
an illusion,
a play on light,
all in my mind.
All these versions of me
exact copies,
they move in sync
endlessly.

If I had the opportunity,
to be a different me,
would I be?
Or would this world
make me the same
all over again?

This whole room glows fuzzy
in my confusion.
Is the floor tilted or
am I walking sideways?
Why does my head weigh
a hundred thousand pounds?

I usually keep my meds here
on the corner of the desk,
but they are nowhere to be found.

What do I do now?

CATerwaul

"Are you ok in there?" they call.
"Did I hear you come back?"
It's Cat calling through the wall.
Their footsteps pace the wood floor hall.
What do they mean *come back*?
They knock and pound and caterwaul.

I stay silent through it all.
My brain traps my words inside.
Cat keeps calling through the wall.
The mirror cracked from the fall
and a million of me watch me do nothing
as Cat knocks and pounds and caterwauls.

The reflections follow me from the desk to the wall.
I write a message on the mirror pane and
Cat keeps calling through the wall.
If only one reflection could overhaul
me, and replace me, and save me from me
as Cat keeps calling from the hall.
They knock and pound and caterwaul.

The Door ... Again

Cat's knocks grow
so much louder
than before,
a crescendo of panic.

"Destiny!
Open up!
Or I have to let myself in!"

Again, I say nothing.
All my words trap
inside my head
like thousands of fish
caught in a net.
The doorknob rustles
like someone who is upset
trying to insert a key
into a tiny hole,
at a moment when
time is of the essence.
I watch it all as if this isn't
happening to me,
like it's somebody else,
maybe one of the other
girls from the mirror.

The door opens.
First just a crack.
Cat pokes their head inside.
They scan the room as if
they are worried about
what they'll find.
Then relief floods their face.
They let out a big loud sigh.

"Why didn't you answer me?"
they say, but their words are
muffled through this fog I'm in.
"Hey are you ok?"

They rush in.
And on instinct
I rush away.
Out the dorm.
Into the night.

17

Brewen

Waking Up

in a park for the first time
on a late September morning
is jarring.
The only thing good about today
is knowing I have somewhere to be,
even if it's work.
It's a relief
to know that there's someone
or someplace
that might be
looking for me.

The Muddiest Waters

Everything is weird
between Kyler and me.
It's clear he doesn't want to talk to me.
He's just too nice to say.
Minutes last for hours
wading through
these muddy waters
without a clear head
or a clear friend.
Alone in a room full of people,
I'm a droid filling shots of espresso.
The patrons don't care if I smile or not.
They just care about their coffees
and if they have whole milk
or skim.
Not long after the cafe closes
while we stack the chairs,

he says, "You're not going to say
anything,
are you?"
I think he actually still cares.
He cares if I smile or not.

"About what?" I ask.

"About how you left with that guy,
The one in the green shirt.
I thought you said,
'It's not like that."

"I did.
I mean it's not.
I don't like him.
He's gross.
I was trying to protect a friend."

"Right," he says

and the room starts to spin
like coffee beans
in the grinder.

But the difference between coffee and me
is that coffee takes time to percolate
and drip through the filter.
But my mind has no filter
for what goes in
or what comes out,
nothing to purify it
or slow it down.
Time is relative,
especially when someone starts to shout.
Oh no!
It's me.
I'm the one shouting.
I've stepped outside of myself again.
Please, not now.
Not here!
Not with his eyes watching
as if they want
to help me.
It'd be easier if they were mad
then I would just leave and never come back.
I run out the door
and down the block.
My legs push forward but
I have nowhere to run to anymore.
I have no one to run to anymore.
But my body keeps moving,
a wailing machine sucking air in
and crying it out.
The earth is unmoved by
the force of my feet
pushing me to the shore.

I need to feel small again
so these emotions don't feel so huge.

People

are the greatest source of pain for me
like layers of damaging UV rays
I don't notice
until I'm burnt.
People who leave.
People who try to convince me
that I can trust people
only to eventually prove to me
it's not safe to trust them.
I can't even trust myself.
This is why I don't know how to ask for help.

Destiny.
She was the only one
who was ever truly there for me.
She was there when I couldn't be
there for myself.
She needs to go on without me.
But now there's no one else.

My Destiny is my past
and the only future I can handle
is each
next
breath.
In and out.
In and out.
In and out.

You're Back

                                        "I didn't think I'd see you back
                                           for another round so soon."

His voice floats through
the open wound
of my heart
like some kind of tonic
that burns as it hits
and cleanses the infection.
His eyes are mirrors,
that reflect my pain
through a pane of empathy.

                                                    "Are you alright?"

"Mr. V.,
thank you for the invite but ..."

                                                      "Just sit, child.
                                    You don't have to play any games today."

"Really, I'd rather be..."

                                                               "Alone?
                                    It looks like the last thing you need right now.
                                                          You stink of it."
                                              He kicks the chair out for me
                                                            with his leg.

My body, not my brain,
makes the choice to sit.
"Thanks, I guess?"

                                                   "Want to talk about it?"

Too many words

clog my voice in my throat.
Even if I did want to talk,
I can't.
My head shakes a no
and I look away from him
toward the purple sunset.
Here comes another night
without a home.

So, we sit silent like stars sharing the same sky,
together and alone.
His chess pieces are all lined up,
waiting,
full of the potential to be played,
a hodgepodge of an eclectic collection.
On the dark side
a green knight made of jade
mocks me,
like he's ready to jump through the crowd
and take me out.
On the other side, a new piece,
a crystal pawn,
refracts the rays of the setting sun
casting bursts of prisms
onto the checkered board.
I reach my hand out
as if to catch one.

"You look like you've never seen her before."

"You didn't have this piece the last time we played."

"Huh," he says.
"You would know."

But his eyes tell me that maybe I don't.

Soul Prisms

"Where is the only place
that the past, present, and future
exist at the same time?"

I pull my hand away
from the playful lights
and look at V.
with no answer.

"The human mind.
And all that's past,
and all that's present,
and all that shit barreling down at us in the future
that's a lot for one brain to process.

The good news is
you can't break a soul.
But there are times when
it might need to bend
or stretch
or change
or flex
or
mend.
See, souls are energy,
like light,
charging eternally
in one direction
through time.
And when a soul hits
a certain circumstance,
it's like light through crystal,
or water,
or glass.
It refracts.

And the many different colors
that make up the one
split.
They splinter
onto their own tracks."

Dipping my hand
back into the refraction,
memories flood in
of all the times
my soul collided
with obstacles.
New homes.
New schools.
New people.
New names.
All the times I thought my heart couldn't
handle one more change,
but did.
All the times I felt like a splintered fraction of myself
and someone else stepped in
to help me feel whole.
"How do I get it back?
You know, my soul?
How do I make it whole again?"

He smiles gently at me

like a magician about to share his trick.
Leaning in like it's a secret
between just the two of us,

"That's the thing about prisms," he says.
"They are an illusion.
The light is always whole.
It just changes speed
to bend through the prism.
It's our perception
of the separation of
each color of light,
each refracted beam,
each aspect of your soul."

He removes the crystal pawn
from the light
and the prisms disappear.
The sun sinks
behind the mountains
but I know it's still there.
Still one,
still whole
despite the obstacles.

"She's yours," he says
as he hands me the crystal pawn.

"But V., you need her
to complete your set."

He pulls a penny from his pocket
and places it on her square on the board.

"Mr. Lincoln will stand in for now.

But you do have a point.
None of these pieces

can do it all on their own."

Rolling the crystal in my hand
light dances in its translucent shell
as if it's captured a spectrum
of memories.
Each cut adds to its fascination,
each splinter an identity.
There's my path
through the obstacle.
There's Destiny's.
Maybe love is like light
not something one person can hold.
Obstacles create the illusion
that love is fractured
when it is always whole.
"Thank you," I say
but the words don't seem enough
to convey my gratitude
for his perspective.

"It's getting late."
He glides his pieces into a black velvety satchel.
His chairs and table fold and fit in a bag he swings
over his back.
"Do you have a place to stay?"

"I'm not sure," I say.
"But I have somewhere
I have to go.
I think I need to adjust
the way I play.
I've been all survival
thinking about myself
and how I stay on the board.
But, there are other pieces
that need me
just as much as

I need them."

To Not From

When I rush,
it's usually from
and not to.
I need to find her,
to apologize,
to let her know
that I want to be there for her
the way she's there for me.
I need to mend this schism
between Destiny and me.
Air burns my lungs
as I move through the crowd
up College Street
to the university.
My feet move in time
with the drum circle I pass by
pounding a happy song.
And even though I have nothing,
V. helped me find something.
I think it's hope
or maybe understanding
of some sort of idea
of who I really am,
of who we really are.

CAT Among the Pigeons

"There you are!"
Cat darts quickly
through a gathering of pigeons
who were otherwise minding
their own business.

I stop in my tracks
in part because of the birds
and in part because of Cat.
"I thought for sure you'd want nothing to do with me,"
I say.
I'm not their resident,
not their responsibility.

"I've been looking all over for you,
Destiny!"

My thoughts drown
the rest of Cat's words.
They still think I'm Destiny.
"What do you mean?" I ask.

"You left last night and didn't come back.

"I told you I was going for a walk."

"I mean after that.
When you left again.
Your phone's been ringing in your room all day.
I had to unlock it and go in
to make sure you were safe.
But then you left.
Don't you remember?
And the message on the mirror,
I didn't understand..."

Cat pauses for my answer,
and when they see I can't, they say,
"I'm just so relieved to see you."

"I have to get back!"
This time my feet fly
fueled by despair.
Time pauses
and I don't need the air
because I'm pretty sure
I'm not breathing.

Up the road, through campus,
ascending the stairs,
I reach the door and key in
and find no one there.
Just like Cat said,
her phone is on the chair,
and the message on the mirror,
and the laundry on the floor.

Mirror Mirror

SPLITTING SOULS REFLECT SOULS SPLITTING
PAWN BECOMES QUEEN BECOMES PAWN
NOBODY LEAVING NOBODY
YOU ARE ALL ARE YOU
ALONE

————

Light bounces off the glass
of the mirror reflecting
what is directly in front of it.

It's me.
Just me.
I'm here
alone.

I can't believe
I didn't think
about how she might need me
after what he did
to her,
to me,
to us.
Her soul is split
like the light through an obstacle.
I have to help her
be whole again.

"Oh, good, you made it back.
Cat breathes heavily behind me,
talking to my reflection in the mirror.
"Destiny, you had us all worried."

"Can't you see that I'm not her?
I could never be
as good as her,
so smart,
so sweet,
and loving.
She has done everything in life right
and I just tear it all apart.
I have to find her."
I rip off my mask
and head back out into the night.

Jaded (K)Night

Racing.
Tracing
my steps.
Pacing.
This reality I'm facing,
is she here
or there?

Wheezing.
Grieving,
My chest is heaving.
Can't catch air while I'm weaving
through these crowded streets.
Kyler passes by
and catches my eye.
like he sees my soul's incomplete.

"Brewen, I'm sorry for the way
things ended today...
Hey, are you ok?"

"Uh, yes... and no.
I mean, I don't know.
I don't have time to explain."
Brushing by
I start to cry.
Wish I could tell him why.
Maybe I will someday
if this rook stays in play
and waits for his line to clear.

Searching.
Yearning.
My brain discerning,
How do I find her again?

She's nowhere near the Church Street square.
I head down to the lake.
Following the moonlight,
the stars bright,
the jaded knight
steps into my path
and hollers at me.

"Well, here she is,
that crazy bitch.
At least I got some cash for these."
Then he throws something at me.
My hands catch it on instinct.
It's the empty bottle
of Alprazolam.

I've got to move.
I've got to prove
this knight's got nothing on me.
But I freeze.
And now there's V.
Out of nowhere he steps in between.

"Not this time.
You're going to want
to leave her alone.
Get off my path.
Go home."

And the knight is removed from the board.

Checkmate

                                        "What are you doing out here so late?"
                                                                    asks V.
                                                        "Are you ok?"

"Why does everyone keep asking,
'Am I ok?'
I'm not. I'm not ok."

                                                        "How can I help?

"I can't find my friend.
Have you seen
another girl who looks like me
pass through?"

                            "Not a lot of traffic down here tonight," he says.

"V.,
why do you play chess with me?
These silly games
really aren't all they seem.
I could know all the best strategies
but what does that really get me
if I can't do anything right?"

                                                        "What happened?"

"My friend and I,
we had a fight.
Last night.
I was just trying to help her
but she didn't see it that way.
And now we're split."

                                                        "Well, you're right.

214

Chess won't help you there."

"This world we live in,
it's like a funny little board.
I can't tell if I'm winning
when I don't know who's keeping score.
Forth and back,
back and forth,
and back again.
How do I progress
when I'm always planning for attack?

Endless conflicts
of dark and light.
We all have our own truths
for what is wrong
and what is right.
But what is right?
And what is wrong?"

He says, "It depends who wins
and who writes the song."

"And this is the life that you will win."

"That's right.
And so will you."

"I don't know how to win."

"You have to know
who's on your team," he says.
"Start playing all the pieces."

But I only have two pieces left to play.
An empty bottle of meds
and the crystal pawn.
I turn them over in my hands.
She needs both of these.

And more than them,
she needs me.

Medication

I used to hate the idea
of a bottle of pills
as a solution
because no solution of chemicals
can erase a history.

This bottle of Alprazolam,
she took these religiously
to stave off her panics
and level her body's chemistry.
They helped with her dissociations
and the intensity
of her anxiety.
But she hasn't had them.

I twist the bottle open.
Somehow, he missed one.
There's a small plastic bag inside
with just one more pill.

Destiny's buried in the stress of this new life.
I will find her the only way I know how.
The crystal pawn throws spectrums in the moonlight,
Red – Orange – Yellow – Green – Blue – Indigo - Violet

I raise the pill as if to toast
an end to this splintered night.

One Square at a Time

From the shadows
a figure emerges that looks
like Destiny.
She wanders to the shore.
"Thanks, V.
I think I've found her,"
I whisper
and quietly follow.

A Noble Mind

She stands there like Ophelia
as if she contemplates the water
as a solution to her distress.
She watches with vacant expression
as her feelings ebb on the surface.
It's a Destiny I've never seen before.
I can't tell if she knows I'm here.
Her noble mind
hides behind
a screen of doubt and fear.

               She speaks to my reflection in the water,
                  "I don't know about change,
                       if I can handle this.
                   I don't know about faith,
                       if I can manage it.
                   I don't know about life,
                    if I can get through this.
                   I don't know about love,
                     when I'm missing it."

She feels it all.
I feel it all.
Past, present, future.
Us.
Her.
Me.

This moment,
her reflection,
send me to a distant memory.

End with a Name

There was a name for me
once upon a long time ago.
but then one day
it had to change.

It was the end of fifth grade,
and the classroom looked like
something exploded.
I had exploded.
But I couldn't remember how,
and I couldn't remember why.

My social worker,
The one before Jandro,
took me to a park
while my foster parents packed up all
my things.
"You need a new start,"
she said as she walked me to a stream.
Another new start.
Another goodbye.
Another new school,
new family.
Another place to reinvent
what it meant to
be me.
I think I cried
enough tears to flood
that stream as we sat on
the shore watching the water
flow away from me.

"It all goes in one direction,"
she said. "You know,
the water in the stream.

It doesn't go backward.
Life moves that way, too.
Maybe we can think about
what it means to be you."

The sleeves of my sweatshirt
sopped up the tears from my cheeks.
"I don't know what that means."

She pulled me to where
the water paused in a pool
and pointed to my reflection.
"My heart really aches," she said.
"There should be
someone who is always
there for you."

"Like you?"
I asked.

"I mean always."
She shook her head to say
it couldn't be her.
"Like someone you can lean on
who you know loves you."

My heart winced at the word *love*.

"Do you know who mine is?"
she asked.

"No. Who?"

"Her." She pointed to her own
reflection in the pool.

"That's you," I said.

"We always have ourselves," she said.
"No matter where we are
or what happens.
And we can choose
the thoughts we think
and the choices we make.
You need her," she pointed to
my reflection in the water.
"more than anyone else."

"I don't even like myself,"
I said.

"Well, then, let's talk about her."
She shifted in the direction
of the stream.
"What do you like about her?"

"Isn't she me?"

"Pretend she's someone different.
What should she be like?"

"Maybe all the things
I'm not.
Maybe she likes rainbows.
Maybe she can sing.
Maybe when she gets
upset, she can handle
everything,
or at least
stay calm.
Maybe she trusts the world.
Maybe she has friends.
Maybe she gets good grades.
Maybe she sees what it's like
to be me,
and loves me anyway.

"Can't you be all those things?"

"Me?
No, that's her,
not me."

"But she is you.
Those are all things
you can be."

"I don't know how
to be somebody new."

"What if we call you Destiny?"

"But that's not my name."
I turned to walk away.

"It's part of it.
It's your middle name.
You can still keep Brewen.
Just the order will change."

I watched the girl in the water
and noticed she didn't cry.
There was something soothing
about her, just knowing
she would always be there.
And maybe somehow with her
I could learn to believe
in me.

Somewhere, somehow,
I had drowned that memory,
and Destiny became so much more
than just another part of me,

like we didn't know
we weren't separate entities,
but refractions
of the same
soul.

The Light is Always Whole

"They wanted you to forget me,
but I'm the other side of you,"
I whisper to our reflection.
"But histories don't work like that
they don't disappear because we tell them to.
We can reframe them,
and we can rename them,
but they are a part
of what makes us whole."

"I still need you, Brew.
You are the survivor
and you save me from me.
I am the shallow
and you are the deep.
You see all the things
that I don't see.
You've always stepped in
when the world turns gray.
You take the blame
when my mind breaks away."

Holding the pawn out to her in the moonlight
spectrums sparkle despite the darkness of night.
They float on the water
and reflect in her eyes.
Our eyes.
"Our soul,
it needed to divide
to conquer this life.
But I think I've figured out...
I need your side.
to love myself.
To trust myself.
To unlock this hurt inside."

"I am the past.
You are the present.
We are the future.
Just like light through obstacles,
though it divides

we are always whole.
We are one. We are whole.

Cat at the Water

Cat approaches gently
with just enough noise
to announce their presence
but not too much to startle.

"This is a beautiful spot."

"Yeah, I just needed to think."

"Do you want to talk?"

This is where I would usually say no,
but instead, I say,
"Yeah,
I have a question for you."

"I'm accepting questions."
Cat's warmth nudges my heart
and I make room for them.

"Why do you care?
You've offered me help.
You followed me here.
And you kept at it
even though
I couldn't let you in."

"I could tell you were lost.
You took so much on:
New school,
new place
your internship counting fish,
your job at the coffee shop.
You seemed a bit different
when you had your mask on.

Nervous.
Like you had to have everything
in its place.
Then I saw you with that guy.
And I saw your face.
I knew something was wrong.
And when you didn't come back last night,
and the way you talked like
you were someone else...
I guess I just care.
I'm here if you need help."

"I don't know how to ask for help."

"You don't have to ask.
I'm offering.
You just have to accept it."

"It's a long story.
I don't even know the whole of it."

"I've got time."

"Well, ok. I guess....
There was a name for me,
once upon a long time ago.
It was Brewen.
But they named me Destiny
when they permanently decided
I was never going home
with my bio family.

Brewen was my past,
a clouded memory,
confidential notes in a burnt envelope
from a past they hoped I'd forget.

But I couldn't forget,

not if I burned it,
not if I starved it,
not if I ignored, moved, or ran from it.

She's a part of me.
The part that protects.
And now I realize,
I need all of me.
Every obstacle in my history,
every part of the story of me.

All the parts that make me whole."

18

When We're Whole

Sea Legs

A new experience,
a new perspective,
balance is both sides
shifting
with constant change.
I accept all of my weaknesses.
I accept all of my strengths.
I have so much more strength
than weakness.
But even my weaknesses
make me whole.

There's a boat heading my way
while I wait outside the ECHO Leahy
Center for Lake Champlain.
And that boat sounds like
opportunity,
adventure,
and discovery.

It feels like my future
as I board with the students
and professors off for another day of research.
My sea legs grow stronger
as I trust my whole self
to step toward my future
and catch my balance
on the shoulder
of friends.

Facing Invasive Species

He catches me in the hall
on my way into class.
Our Intro to Marine Biology lab
is due today.

"Yeah, so,
you have our report, right?"
Faris asks as if
nothing's happened.

"I have my report," I say
and look him in the eye
like I've turned full rainbow smelt
wearing my own spectrum of colors
on my thick skin.
I am whole now,
this light knows how to bend.
And right now
what's Brewen in me
won't scurry from
the likes of him.
"I already let Professor Thomsen
know there was an unfortunate incident.
We definitely can't be partners,
and I'm not even sure
if you are allowed to be
in the same class as me.
Did the Dean talk with you yet?"

"Seriously? You didn't?!"

"I did," I say
and my words don't freeze up,
and he can't lead me away.
And I don't panic,

I don't disassociate.
I am whole and assertive.
"So, at the very least,
you sit nowhere near me today."
As Faris walks off,
I see a friendly face
two rows back.
For the first time
I realize
it's Kyler
watching as if
he's been waiting for me
to get to this moment.

"Do you need a new lab partner?" He asks.

As I sit down beside him,
my hips nudge him over
to make room in our seats.

I can't help but think
about how my heart
may be ready
to make room for him, too.

Pawn Promotion

A pawn who plays her way
through all the obstacles
and makes it to the other side
transforms
into a queen.

She can go anywhere,
be anything.

And the funny thing is
she was always a queen.

She just didn't know it yet.

Acknowledgements

If I were to do a gratitude sprint right now, I'd send endless thanks to:

Readers, thank you for giving Brewen a home in your thoughts. I hope these words impacted you in ways you hadn't expected. I hope you feel whole, or at least appreciate all of the separate parts of you.

My Family, for always chasing rainbows and adventures with me, and for understanding how my work isn't something my heart can check at the door.

My boys, Bobby, Liam, and Ceallach, who school me on chess and create alongside me.

My mom and dad, Sally and Mike O'Neill, who made sure I found the songs in my heart, and encourage me to share them with the world.

My husband, Rob, my co-creator of life and family, for your endless love and support.

My sister, Kelly Zieba. You define sisterhood. I modeled the love that Brewen has for Destiny on the love I have for you and April.

My brother, Jon (you made it in the liner notes), for helping me tap into the pulse of the world's rhythms.

Kathy Hoskins and Steven LaBrie, for your professional and foster parent input, for helping me help Brewen Destiny navigate her emancipation from care.

Joe Hudson, my partner in compassion, as we support each other in supporting others in their times of panic and dissociation. The world knows no more dependable heart than yours.

My Trinity College of VT sisters, it's been a long time, but I can't think of Burlington without thinking of you. Collectively, you may find some Easter eggs of our experiences from once upon a time.

Carrie Jones and Jenna Pashley, for your time and developmental input on the storyline and the structure of my poems. Your creativity and kindness are boundless.

Jess Keating, for your Epic Author's Academy where you spoke of soul prisms and compressing time. My thoughts welled over with the realization that I have been writing this story for years, I just didn't know it yet.

To all of the educators I've worked with who would give their crystal unicorn to provide a rainbow of calm for a student with OCD.

To every student and person I've worked with, you've maintained a beautiful soul through challenging changes, moments and systems. You are the real life versions of Destiny and Victorious. There is a special place in my heart for you.

Betsy O'Neill-Sheehan is a lifelong student of human story, and how our inner narratives shape who we are and what we can become. As a school counselor and therapeutic social worker, she is passionate about helping others discover the strengths and love in themselves.

FIND YOUR TRUTHS.
WRITE YOUR SONGS.